THEY HAVE A CLUB AND I AM NOT IN IT. IT IS ALSO A
CLUB AGAINST ME. THEY ARE REALLY OUT TO GET ME.
I HAVE NEVER HAD TO GO THROUGH SOMETHING LIKE
THIS. I WILL HAVE TO BE VERY BRAVE. I WILL NEVER
GIVE UP THIS NOTEBOOK BUT IT IS CLEAR THAT THEY
ARE GOING TO BE AS MEAN AS THEY CAN UNTIL I DO.
THEY JUST DON'T KNOW HARRIET M. WELSCH.

LOUISE FITZHUGH's best-known novels, *Harriet the
Spy* and *The Long Secret,* have been acclaimed as
milestones in the world of children's literature.
Known for their wry detail and lively drawings, the
two books have become international best-sellers.
Born in Memphis, Tennessee, in 1928, the author
was a multi-talented person. She studied painting at
the Art Students League in New York City and in
Bologna, Italy, and was widely recognized as an
artist. Louise Fitzhugh died in 1974.

Written and
Illustrated by
LOUISE FITZHUGH

HARRIET
THE SPY

LAUREL-LEAF BOOKS bring together under a single imprint out-standing works of fiction and nonfiction particularly suitable for young adult readers, both in and out of the classroom. Charles F. Reasoner, Professor Emeritus of Children's Literature and Reading, New York University, is consultant to this series.

Published by
Dell Publishing Co., Inc.
1 Dag Hammarskjold Plaza
New York, New York 10017

Laurel-Leaf Library ® TM 766734, Dell Publishing Co., Inc.

ISBN: 0-440-93447-8

RL: 5.2

Reprinted by arrangement with Harper & Row, Publishers, Inc.
Printed in the United States of America
First Laurel-Leaf printing—June 1978
Eleventh Laurel-Leaf printing—November 1984

BOOK ONE

CHAPTER 1

Harriet was trying to explain to Sport how to play Town. "See, first you make up the name of the town. Then you write down the names of all the people who live in it. You can't have too many or it gets too hard. I usually have twenty-five."

"Ummmm." Sport was tossing a football in the air. They were in the courtyard of Harriet's house on East Eighty-seventh Street in Manhattan.

"Then when you know who lives there, you make up what they do. For instance, Mr. Charles Hanley runs the filling station on the corner." Harriet spoke thoughtfully as she squatted next to the big tree, bending so low over her notebook that her long straight hair touched the edges.

"Don'tcha wanta play football?" Sport asked.

"Now, listen, Sport, you never did this and it's fun. Now over here next to this curve in the mountain we'll put the filling station. So if anything happens there, you remember where it is."

Sport tucked the football under his arm and walked over to her. "That's nothing but an old tree root. Whaddya mean, a mountain?"

"That's a mountain. From now on that's a mountain. Got it?" Harriet looked up into his face.

Sport moved back a pace. "Looks like an old tree root," he muttered.

Harriet pushed her hair back and looked at him seriously. "Sport, what are you going to be when you grow up?"

"You know what. You know I'm going to be a ball player."

"Well, I'm going to be a writer. And when I say that's a mountain, that's a mountain." Satisfied, she turned back to her town.

Sport put the football gently on the ground and knelt beside her, looking over her shoulder at the notebook in which she scribbled furiously.

"Now, as soon as you've got all the men's names down, and their wives' names and their children's names, then you figure out all their professions. You've got to have a doctor, a lawyer—"

"And an Indian chief," Sport interrupted.

"No. Someone who works in television."

"What makes you think they have television?"

"I say they do. And, anyway, my father has to be in it, doesn't he?"

"Well, then put mine in too. Put a writer in it."

"Okay, we can make Mr. Jonathan Fishbein a writer."

"And let him have a son like me who cooks for him." Sport rocked back and forth on his heels, chanting in singsong, "And let him be eleven years old like me, and let him have a mother who went away and has all the money, and let him grow up to be a ball player."

"Nooo," Harriet said in disgust. "Then you're not making it up. Don't you understand?"

Sport paused. "No," he said.

"Just listen, Sport. See, now that we have all this

written down, I'll show you where the fun is." Harriet got very businesslike. She stood up, then got on her knees in the soft September mud so she could lean over the little valley made between the two big roots of the tree. She referred to her notebook every now and then, but for the most part she stared intently at the mossy lowlands which made her town. "Now, one night, late at night, Mr. Charles Hanley is in his filling station. He is just about to turn out the lights and go home because it is nine o'clock and time for him to get ready for bed."

"But he's a grown-up!" Sport looked intently at the spot occupied by the gas station.

"In this town everybody goes to bed at nine-thirty," Harriet said definitely.

"Oh"—Sport rocked a little on his heels—"my father goes to bed at nine in the morning. Sometimes I meet him getting up."

"And also, Dr. Jones is delivering a baby to Mrs. Harrison right over here in the hospital. Here is the hospital, the Carterville General Hospital." She pointed to the other side of town. Sport looked at the left root.

"What is Mr. Fishbein, the writer, doing?"

Harriet pointed to the center of town. "He is in the town bar, which is right here." Harriet looked down at the town as though hypnotized. "Here's what happens. Now, this night, as Mr. Hanley is just about to close up, a long, big old black car drives up and in it there are all these men with guns. They drive in real fast and Mr. Hanley gets scared. They jump out of the car and run over and rob Mr. Hanley, who is petrified. They steal all the money in the gas station, then they fill up with gas free and then they zoom off in the night. Mr. Hanley is all bound and gagged on the floor."

Sport's mouth hung open. "Then what?"

9

"At this same minute Mrs. Harrison's baby is born and Dr. Jones says, 'You have a fine baby girl, Mrs. Harrison, a fine baby girl, ho, ho, ho.' "

"Make it a boy."

"No, it's a girl. She already has a boy."

"What does the baby look like?"

"She's ugly. Now, also at this very minute, on the other side of town, over here past the gas station, almost to the mountain, the robbers have stopped at a farmhouse which belongs to Ole Farmer Dodge. They go in and find him eating oatmeal because he doesn't have any teeth. They throw the oatmeal on the floor and demand some other food. He doesn't have anything but oatmeal, so they beat him up. Then they settle down to spend the night. Now, at this very minute, the police chief of Carterville, who is called Chief Herbert, takes a stroll down the main street. He senses something is not right and he wonders what it is. . . ."

"Harriet. Get up out of that mud." A harsh voice rang out from the third floor of the brownstone behind them.

Harriet looked up. There was a hint of anxiety in her face. "Oh, Ole Golly, I'm not in the mud."

The face of the nurse looking out of the window was not the best-looking face in the world, but for all its frowning, its sharp, dark lines, there was kindness there. "Harriet M. Welsch, you are to rise to your feet."

Harriet rose without hesitation. "But, listen, we'll have to play Town standing up," she said plaintively.

"That's the best way" came back sharply, and the head disappeared.

Sport stood up too. "Why don't we play football, then?"

"No, look, if I just sit like this I won't be in the

10

mud." So saying, she squatted on her heels next to the town. "Now, he senses that there is something wrong—"

"How can he? He hasn't seen anything and it's all on the other side of town."

"He just feels it. He's a very *good* police chief."

"Well," Sport said dubiously.

"So, since he's the only policeman in town, he goes around and deputizes everybody and he says to them, 'Something is fishy in this here town. I feel it in my bones,' and everybody follows him and they get on their horses—"

"Horses!" Sport shrieked.

"They get in the squad car and they drive around town until—"

"Harriet." The back door slammed and Ole Golly marched squarely toward them across the yard. Her long black shoes made a slap-slap noise on the brick.

"Hey, where are you going?" asked Harriet, jumping up. Because Ole Golly had on her outdoor things. Ole Golly just had indoor things and outdoor things. She never wore anything as recognizable as a skirt, a jacket, or a sweater. She just had yards and yards of tweed which enveloped her like a lot of discarded blankets, which ballooned out when she walked, and which she referred to as her Things.

"I'm going to take you somewhere. It's time you began to see the world. You're eleven years old and it's time you saw something." She stood there above them, so tall that when they looked up they saw the blue sky behind her head.

Harriet felt a twinge of guilt because she had seen a lot more than Ole Golly thought she had. But all she said was, "Oh, boy," and jumped up and down.

"Get your coat and hurry. We're leaving right now." Ole Golly always did everything right now. "Come on, Sport, it won't hurt you to look around too."

"I have to be back at seven to cook dinner." Sport jumped up as he said this.

"We'll be back long before that. Harriet and I eat at six. Why do you eat so late?"

"He has cocktails first. I have olives and peanuts."

"That's nice. Now go get your coats."

Sport and Harriet ran through the back door, slamming it behind them.

"What's all the noise?" spluttered the cook, who whirled around just in time to see them fly through the kitchen door and up the back stairs. Harriet's room was at the top of the house, so they had three flights to run up and they were breathless by the time they got there.

"Where're we going?" Sport shouted after Harriet's flying feet.

"I don't know," Harriet panted as they entered her room, "but Ole Golly always has good places."

Sport grabbed his coat and was out the door and halfway down the steps when Harriet said, "Wait, wait, I can't find my notebook."

"Oh, whadya need that for?" Sport yelled from the steps.

"I never go anywhere without it," came the muffled answer.

"Aw, come on, Harriet." There were great crashing noises coming from the bedroom. "Harriet? Did you fall down?"

A muffled but very relieved voice came out. "I found it. It must have slipped behind the bed." And Harriet emerged clutching a green composition book.

"You must have a hundred of them now," Sport said as they went down the steps.

"No, I have fourteen. This is number fifteen. How could I have a hundred? I've only been working since I was eight, and I'm only eleven now. I wouldn't even

12

have this many except at first I wrote so big my regular route took almost the whole book."

"You see the same people every day?"

"Yes. This year I have the Dei Santi family, Little Joe Curry, the Robinsons, Harrison Withers, and a new one, Mrs. Plumber. Mrs. Plumber is the hardest because I have to get in the dumbwaiter."

"Can I go with you sometime?"

"No, silly. Spies don't go with friends. Anyway, we'd get caught if there were two of us. Why don't you get your own route?"

"Sometimes I watch out my window a window across the way."

"What happens there?"

"Nothing. A man comes home and pulls the shade down."

"That's not very exciting."

"It sure isn't."

They met Ole Golly waiting for them, tapping her foot, outside the front door. They walked to Eighty-sixth Street, took the crosstown bus, and soon were whizzing along in the subway, sitting in a line—Ole Golly, then Harriet, then Sport. Ole Golly stared straight ahead. Harriet was scribbling furiously in her notebook.

"What are you writing?" Sport asked.

"I'm taking notes on all those people who are sitting over there."

"Why?"

"Aw, Sport"—Harriet was exasperated—"because I've *seen* them and I want to *remember* them." She turned back to her book and continued her notes:

MAN WITH ROLLED WHITE SOCKS, FAT LEGS. WOMAN WITH ONE CROSS-EYE AND A LONG NOSE. HORRIBLE LOOKING LITTLE BOY AND A FAT BLONDE MOTHER WHO KEEPS WIPING HIS NOSE OFF. FUNNY LADY LOOKS LIKE

A TEACHER AND IS READING. I DON'T THINK I'D LIKE TO LIVE WHERE ANY OF THESE PEOPLE LIVE OR DO THE THINGS THEY DO. I BET THAT LITTLE BOY IS SAD AND CRIES A LOT. I BET THAT LADY WITH THE CROSS-EYE LOOKS IN THE MIRROR AND JUST FEELS TERRIBLE.

Ole Golly leaned over and spoke to them. "We're going to Far Rockaway. It's about three stops from here. I want you to see how this person lives, Harriet. This is *my* family."

Harriet almost gasped. She looked up at Ole Golly in astonishment, but Ole Golly just stared out the window again. Harriet continued to write:

THIS IS INCREDIBLE. COULD OLE GOLLY HAVE A FAMILY? I NEVER THOUGHT ABOUT IT. HOW COULD OLE GOLLY HAVE A MOTHER AND FATHER? SHE'S TOO OLD FOR ONE THING AND SHE'S NEVER SAID ONE WORD ABOUT THEM AND I'VE KNOWN HER SINCE I WAS BORN. ALSO SHE DOESN'T GET ANY LETTERS. THINK ABOUT THIS. THIS MIGHT BE IMPORTANT.

They came to their stop and Ole Golly led them off the subway.

"Gee," said Sport as they came up onto the sidewalk, "we're near the ocean." And they could smell it, the salt, and even a wild soft spray which blew gently across their faces, then was gone.

"Yes," said Ole Golly briskly. Harriet could see a change in her. She walked faster and held her head higher.

They were walking down a street that led to the water. The houses, set back from the sidewalk with a patch of green in front, were built of yellow brick interspersed with red. It wasn't very pretty, Harriet thought, but maybe they liked their houses this way, better than those plain red brick ones in New York.

Ole Golly was walking faster and looking sterner. She looked as though she wished she hadn't come. Abruptly she turned in at a sidewalk leading to a house. She strode relentlessly up the steps, never looking back, never saying a word. Sport and Harriet followed, wide-eyed, up the steps to the front door, through the front hall, and out the back door.

She's lost her mind, Harriet thought. She and Sport looked at each other with raised eyebrows. Then they saw that Ole Golly was heading for a small private house which sat in its own garden behind the apartment house. Harriet and Sport stood still, not knowing what to do. This little house was like a house in the country, the kind Harriet saw when she went to Water Mill in the summer. The unpainted front had the same soft gray of driftwood, the roof a darker gray.

"Come on, chickens, let's get us a hot cup of tea." Ole Golly, suddenly gay, waved from the funny little rotting porch.

Harriet and Sport ran toward the house, but stopped cold when the front door opened with a loud swish. There, suddenly, was the largest woman Harriet had ever seen.

"Why, lookahere what's coming," she bellowed, "looka them lil rascals," and her great fat face crinkled into large cheerful lumps as her mouth split to show a toothless grin. She let forth a high burbling laugh.

Sport and Harriet stood staring, their mouths open. The fat lady stood like a mountain, her hands on her hips, in a flowered cotton print dress and enormous hanging coat sweater. Probably the biggest sweater in the world, thought Harriet; probably the biggest pair of shoes too. And her shoes were a wonder. Long, long, black, bumpy things with high, laced sides up to the middle of the shin, bulging with the effort of holding in those ankles, their laces splitting them

15

into grins against the white of the socks below. Harriet fairly itched to takes notes on her.

"Wherecha get these lil things?" Her cheer rang out all over the neighborhood. "This the lil Welsch baby? That her brother?"

Sport giggled.

"No, it's my husband," Harriet shouted.

Ole Golly turned a grim face. "Don't be snarky, Harriet, and don't think you're such a wit either."

The fat lady laughed, making her face fall in lumps again. She looks like dough, Harriet thought, about to be made into a big round Italian loaf. She wanted to tell Sport this, but Ole Golly was leading them in, all of them squeezing past that mountain of a stomach because the fat lady stood, rather stupidly, in the doorway.

Ole Golly marched to the teakettle and put a fire under it. Then she turned in a businesslike way and introduced them. "Children, this is my mother, Mrs. Golly. Mother—you can close the door now, Mother. This is Harriet Welsch."

"Harriet M. Welsch," Harriet corrected.

"You know perfectly well you have no middle name, but if you insist, Harriet M. Welsch. And this is Sport. What's your last name, Sport?"

"Rocque. Simon Rocque." He pronounced it Rock.

"Simon, Simon, hee, hee, hee." Harriet felt very ugly all of a sudden.

"You are not to make fun of anyone's name." Ole Golly loomed over Harriet and it was one of those times when Harriet knew she meant it.

"I take it back," Harriet said quickly.

"That's better." Ole Golly turned away cheerfully. "Now let's all sit down and have some tea."

"Waal, ain't she a cute lil thing." Harriet could see that Mrs. Golly was still hung up on the introduc-

16

tions. She stood like a mountain, her big ham hands dangling helplessly at her sides.

"Sit down, Mother," Ole Golly said gently, and Mrs. Golly sat.

Harriet and Sport looked at each other. The same thought was occurring to both of them. This fat lady wasn't very bright.

Mrs. Golly sat to the left of Harriet. She leaned over Harriet, in fact, and looked directly into her eyes. Harriet felt like something in a zoo.

"Now, Harriet, look around you," Ole Golly said sternly as she poured the tea. "I brought you here because you've never seen the inside of a house like this. Have you ever seen a house that has one bed, one table, four chairs, and a bathtub in the kitchen?"

Harriet had to move her chair back to see around Mrs. Golly, who leaned toward her, motionless, still looking. The room *was* a strange one. There was a sad little rug next to the stove. Harrison Withers has only a bed and a table, Harriet thought to herself. But since she didn't want Ole Golly to know she had been peering through Harrison Withers' skylight, she said nothing.

"I didn't think you had," said Ole Golly. "Look around. And drink your tea, children. You may have more milk and sugar if I haven't put enough."

"I don't drink tea," Sport said timidly.

Ole Golly shot an eye at him. "What do you mean you don't drink tea?"

"I mean I never have."

"You mean you've never tasted it?"

"No," said Sport and looked a little terrified.

Harriet looked at Ole Golly. Ole Golly wore an arch expression which signified that she was about to quote.

" 'There are few hours in life more agreeable than the hour dedicated to the ceremony known as after-

18

noon tea.' " Ole Golly said this steadily and sedately, then leaned back in her chair with a satisfied look at Sport. Sport looked completely blank.

"Henry James," said Ole Golly, "1843-1916. From *Portrait of a Lady*."

"What's that?" Sport asked Harriet.

"A novel, silly," said Harriet.

"Oh, like my father writes," said Sport, and dismissed the whole thing.

"My dotter's a smart one," mumbled Mrs. Golly, still looking straight at Harriet.

"Behold, Harriet," Ole Golly said, "a woman who never had any interest in anyone else, nor in any book, nor in any school, nor in any way of life, but has lived her whole life in this room, eating and sleeping and waiting to die."

Harriet stared at Mrs. Golly in horror. Should Ole Golly be saying these things? Wouldn't Mrs. Golly get mad? But Mrs. Golly just sat looking contentedly at Harriet. Perhaps, thought Harriet, she forgets to turn her head away from something unless she is told.

"Try it, Sport, it's good." Harriet spoke to Sport quickly in an effort to change the subject.

Sport took a sip. "It's not bad," he said weakly.

"Try everything, Sport, at least once." Ole Golly said this as though her mind weren't really on it. Harriet looked at her curiously. Ole Golly was acting very strangely indeed. She seemed . . . was she angry? No, not angry. She seemed sad. Harriet realized with a start that it was the first time she had ever seen Ole Golly look sad. She hadn't even known Ole Golly *could* be sad.

Almost as though she were thinking the same thing, Ole Golly suddenly shook her head and sat up straight. "Well," she said brightly, "I think we have had enough tea and enough sights for one day. I

19

think we had better go home now."

The most extraordinary thing happened next. Mrs. Golly leaped to her fat feet and threw her teacup down on the floor. "You're always leaving. You're always leaving," she screamed.

"Now, Mother," Ole Golly said calmly.

Mrs. Golly hopped around the middle of the floor like a giant doll. She made Harriet think of those balloons, blown up like people, that bounce on the end of a string. Sport giggled suddenly. Harriet felt like giggling but wasn't sure she should.

Mrs. Golly bobbed away. "Just come here to leave me again. Always leaving. Thought you'd come for good this time."

"Now, Mother," Ole Golly said again, but this time got to her feet, walked to her mother, and laid a firm hand on the bouncing shoulder. "Mother," she said gently, "you know I'll be here next week."

"Oh, that's right," said Mrs. Golly. She stopped jumping immediately and gave a big smile to Harriet and Sport.

"Oh, boy," said Sport under his breath.

Harriet sat fascinated. Then Ole Golly got them all bundled into their clothes and they were outside on the street again, having waved to a cheerful Mrs. Golly. They walked along through the darkening day.

"Boy, oh, boy" was all Sport could say.

Harriet couldn't wait to get back to her room to finish her notes.

Ole Golly looked steadily ahead. There was no expression on her face at all.

CHAPTER 2

When Harriet was ready for bed that night, she took out her notebook. She had a lot to think about. Tomorrow was the beginning of school. Tomorrow she would have a quantity of notes to take on the changes that had taken place in her friends over the summer. Tonight she wanted to think about Mrs. Golly.

I THINK THAT LOOKING AT MRS. GOLLY MUST MAKE OLE GOLLY SAD. MY MOTHER ISN'T AS SMART AS OLE GOLLY BUT SHE'S NOT AS DUMB AS MRS. GOLLY. I WOULDN'T LIKE TO HAVE A DUMB MOTHER. IT MUST MAKE YOU FEEL VERY UNPOPULAR. I THINK I WOULD LIKE TO WRITE A STORY ABOUT MRS. GOLLY GETTING RUN OVER BY A TRUCK EXCEPT SHE'S SO FAT I WONDER WHAT WOULD HAPPEN TO THE TRUCK. I HAD BETTER CHECK ON THAT. I WOULD NOT LIKE TO LIVE LIKE MRS. GOLLY BUT I WOULD LIKE TO KNOW WHAT GOES ON IN HER HEAD.

Harriet put the book down and ran in to Ole Golly's room to kiss her good night. Ole Golly sat in a rocker in the light of an overhead lamp, reading. Harriet flew

21

into the room and bounded right into the center of the billowy yellow quilt which covered the single bed. Everything in the room was yellow, from the walls to the vase of chrysanthemums. Ole Golly "took to" yellow, as she put it.

"Take your feet off the bed," Ole Golly said without looking up.

"What does your mother think about?" asked Harriet.

"I don't know," said Ole Golly in a musing way, still looking at her book. "I've wondered that for years.",

"What are you reading?" Harriet asked.

"Dostoievsky."

"What's *that?*" asked Harriet in a thoroughly obnoxious way.

"Listen to this," Ole Golly said and got that quote look on her face: " 'Love all God's creation, the whole and every grain of sand in it. Love every leaf, every ray of God's light. Love the animals, love the plants, love everything. If you love everything, you will perceive the divine mystery in things. Once you perceive it, you will begin to comprehend it better every day. And you will come at last to love the whole world with an all-embracing love.' "

"What does that mean?" Harriet asked after she had been quiet a minute. "What do you think it means?"

"Well, maybe if you love everything, then . . . then —I guess you'll know everything . . . then . . . seems like . . . you love everything more. I don't know. Well, that's about it. . . ." Ole Golly looked at Harriet in as gentle a way as she could considering the fact that her face looked like it was cut out of oak.

"I want to know everything, everything," screeched Harriet suddenly, lying back and bouncing up and down on the bed. "Everything in the world, everything, everything. I will be a spy and know everything."

"It won't do you a bit of good to know everything if you don't do anything with it. Now get up, Miss Harriet the Spy, you're going to sleep now." And with that Ole Golly marched over and grabbed Harriet by the ear.

"Ouch," said Harriet as she was led to her room, but it really didn't hurt.

"There now, into bed."

"Will Mommy and Daddy be home in time to kiss me good night?"

"They will not," said Ole Golly as she tucked Harriet in. "They went to a party. You'll see them in the morning at breakfast. Now to sleep, instantly—"

"Hee, hee," said Harriet, "instant sleep."

"And not another word out of you. Tomorrow you go back to school." Ole Golly leaned over and gave her a hard little peck on the forehead. Ole Golly was never very kissy, which Harriet thought was just as well, as she hated it. Ole Golly turned the light out and Harriet listened to her go back into her room which was right across the hall, pick up her book, and sit down in the rocker again. Then Harriet did what she always did when she was supposed to be asleep. She got out her flashlight, put the book she was currently reading under the covers, and read happily until Ole Golly came in and took the flashlight away as she did every night.

The next morning Mrs. Welsch asked, "Wouldn't you like to try a ham sandwich, or egg salad, or peanut butter?" Her mother looked quizzically at Harriet while the cook stood next to the table looking enraged.

"Tomato," said Harriet, not even looking up from the book she was reading at breakfast.

"Stop reading at the table." Harriet put the book down. "Listen, Harriet, you've taken a tomato sandwich to school every day for five years. Don't you get tired of them?"

"No."

"How about cream cheese and olive?"

Harriet shook her head. The cook threw up one arm in despair.

"Pastrami? Roast beef? Cucumber?"

"Tomato."

Mrs. Welsch raised her shoulders and looked helplessly at the cook. The cook grimaced. "Sot in her ways," the cook said firmly and left the room. Mrs. Welsch took a sip of coffee. "Are you looking forward to school?"

"Not particularly."

Mr. Welsch put the paper down and looked at his daughter. "Do you like school?"

"No," said Harriet.

"I always hated it," said Mr. Welsch and went back behind the paper.

"Dear, you mustn't say things like that. I rather liked it—that is, when I was eleven I did." Mrs. Welsch looked at Harriet as though expecting an answer.

Harriet didn't know what she felt about school.

"Drink your milk," said Mrs. Welsch. Harriet always waited until her mother said this, no matter how thirsty she was. It made her feel comfortable to have her mother remind her. She drank her milk, wiped her mouth sedately, and got up from the table. Ole Golly came into the room on her way to the kitchen.

"What do you say when you get up from the table, Harriet?" Mrs. Welsch asked absent-mindedly.

"Excuse me," said Harriet.

"Good manners are very important, particularly in the morning," snapped Ole Golly as she went through the door. Ole Golly was always horribly grumpy in the morning.

Harriet ran very fast all the way up to her room.

"I'm starting the sixth grade," she yelled, just to keep herself company. She got her notebook, slammed her door, and thundered down the steps. "Good-by, good-by," she yelled, as though she were going to Africa, and slammed out the front door.

Harriet's school was called The Gregory School, having been founded by a Miss Eleanore Gregory around the turn of the century. It was on East End Avenue, a few blocks from Harriet's house and across the street from Carl Schurz Park. Harriet skipped away down East End Avenue, hugging her notebook happily.

At the entrance to her school a group of children crowded through the door. More stood around on the sidewalk. They were all shapes and sizes and mostly girls because The Gregory School was a girl's school. Boys were allowed to attend up through the sixth grade, but after that they had to go someplace else. It made Harriet sad to think that after this year Sport wouldn't be in school. She didn't care about the others. In particular about Pinky Whitehead she didn't care, because she thought he was the dumbest thing in the world. The only other boy in her class was a boy Harriet had christened The Boy with the Purple Socks, because he was so boring no one ever bothered to remember his name. He had come to the school last year and everyone else had been there since the first grade. Harriet remembered that first day when he had come in with those purple socks on. Whoever heard of purple socks? She figured it was lucky he wore them; otherwise no one would have even known he was there at all. He never said a word.

Sport came up to her as she leaned against a fire hydrant and opened her notebook. "Hi," he said.

"Hi."

"Anyone else here yet?"

"Just that dumb boy with the purple socks."

Harriet wrote quickly in her notebook:

26

SOMETIMES SPORT LOOKS AS THOUGH HE'S BEEN UP ALL NIGHT. HE HAS FUNNY LITTLE DRY THINGS AROUND HIS EYES. I WORRY ABOUT HIM.

"Sport, did you wash your face?"

"Huh? Uh . . . no, I forgot."

"Hmmmm," Harriet said disapprovingly, and Sport looked away. Actually Harriet hadn't washed hers either, but you couldn't tell it.

"Hey, there's Janie." Sport pointed up the street.

Janie Gibbs was Harriet's best friend besides Sport. She had a chemistry set and planned one day to blow up the world. Both Harriet and Sport had a great respect for Janie's experiments, but they didn't understand a word she said about them.

Janie came slowly toward them, her eyes apparently focused on a tree across the street in the park. She looked odd walking that way, her head turned completely to the right like a soldier on parade. Both Sport and Harriet knew she did this because she was shy and didn't want to see anyone, so they didn't mention it.

She almost bumped into them.

"Hi."

"Hi."

"Hi."

That over, they all stood there.

"Oh, dear," said Janie, "another year. Another year older and I'm no closer to my goal."

Sport and Harriet nodded seriously. They watched a long black limousine driven by a chauffeur. It stopped in front of the school. A small blonde girl got out.

"There's that dreadful Beth Ellen Hansen," said Janie with a sneer. Beth Ellen was the prettiest girl in the class, so everyone despised her, particularly Janie, who was rather plain and freckled.

27

Harriet took some notes:

JANIE GETS STRANGER EVERY YEAR. I THINK SHE MIGHT BLOW UP THE WORLD. BETH ELLEN ALWAYS LOOKS LIKE SHE MIGHT CRY.

Rachel Hennessey and Marion Hawthorne came walking up together. They were always together. "Good morning, Harriet, Simon, Jane," Marion Hawthorne said very formally. She acted like a teacher, as though she were one minute from rapping on the desk for attention. Rachel did everything Marion did, so now she looked down her nose at them and nodded hello, one quick jerk of the head. The two of them went into the school then.

"Are they not too much?" Janie said and looked away in disgust.

Carrie Andrews got off the bus. Harriet wrote:

CARRIE ANDREWS IS CONSIDERABLY FATTER THIS YEAR.

Laura Peters got out of the station wagon bus. Harriet wrote:

AND LAURA PETERS IS THINNER AND UGLIER. I THINK SHE COULD USE SOME BRACES ON HER TEETH.

"Oh, boy," said Sport. They looked and there was Pinky Whitehead. Pinky was so pale, thin, and weak that he looked like a glass of milk, a tall thin glass of milk. Sport couldn't bear to look at him. Harriet turned away from habit, then looked back to see if he had changed. Then she wrote:

PINKY WHITEHEAD HAS NOT CHANGED. PINKY WHITE-HEAD WILL NEVER CHANGE.

Harriet consulted her mental notes on Pinky. He lived on Eighty-eighth Street. He had a very beautiful mother, a father who worked on a magazine, and a baby sister three years old. Harriet wrote:

MY MOTHER IS ALWAYS SAYING PINKY WHITEHEAD'S WHOLE PROBLEM IS HIS MOTHER. I BETTER ASK HER WHAT THAT MEANS OR I'LL NEVER FIND OUT. DOES HIS MOTHER HATE HIM? IF I HAD HIM I'D HATE HIM.

"Well, it's time to go in," said Sport in a tired voice.

"Yeah, let's get this over with," said Janie and turned toward the door.

Harriet closed her notebook and they all went in. Their first period was Assembly in the big study hall.

Miss Angela Whitehead, the present dean, stood at the podium. Harriet scribbled in her notebook as soon as she took her seat:

MISS WHITEHEAD'S FEET LOOK LARGER THIS YEAR. MISS WHITEHEAD HAS BUCK TEETH, THIN HAIR, FEET LIKE SKIS, AND A VERY LONG HANGING STOMACH. OLE GOLLY SAYS DESCRIPTION IS GOOD FOR THE SOUL AND CLEARS THE BRAIN LIKE A LAXATIVE. THAT SHOULD TAKE CARE OF MISS WHITEHEAD.

"Good morning, children." Miss Whitehead bowed as gracefully as a pussy willow. The students rose in a shuffling body. "Good morning, Miss Whitehead," they intoned, an undercurrent of grumbling rising immediately afterward like a second theme. Miss Whitehead made a short speech about gum and candy wrappers being thrown all over the school. She didn't see any reason for this. Then followed the readings. Every morning two or three older girls read short passages from books, usually the Bible. Harriet never listened.

She got enough quotes from Ole Golly. She used this time to write in her book:

OLE GOLLY SAYS THERE IS AS MANY WAYS TO LIVE AS THERE ARE PEOPLE ON THE EARTH AND I SHOULDN'T GO ROUND WITH BLINDERS BUT SHOULD SEE EVERY WAY I CAN. THEN I'LL KNOW WHAT WAY I WANT TO LIVE AND NOT JUST LIVE LIKE MY FAMILY.

I'LL TELL YOU ONE THING, I DON'T WANT TO LIVE LIKE MISS WHITEHEAD. THE OTHER DAY I SAW HER IN THE GROCERY STORE AND SHE BOUGHT ONE SMALL CAN OF TUNA, ONE DIET COLA, AND A PACKAGE OF CIGARETTES. NOT EVEN ONE TOMATO. SHE MUST HAVE A TERRIBLE LIFE. I CAN'T WAIT TO GET BACK TO MY REGULAR SPY ROUTE THIS AFTERNOON. I'VE BEEN AWAY ALL SUMMER AND THOSE HOUSES IN THE COUNTRY ARE TOO FAR AWAY FROM EACH OTHER. TO GET MUCH DONE I WOULD HAVE TO DRIVE.

Assembly was over. The class got up and filed into the sixth-grade room. Harriet grabbed a desk right across the aisle one way from Sport and the other way from Janie.

"Hey!" Sport said because he was glad. If they hadn't been able to grab these desks, it would have been hard passing notes.

Miss Elson stood at her desk. She was their homeroom teacher. Harriet looked at her curiously, then wrote:

I THINK MISS ELSON IS ONE OF THOSE PEOPLE YOU DON'T BOTHER TO THINK ABOUT TWICE.

She slammed the notebook shut as though she had put Miss Elson in a box and slammed the lid. Miss Elson called the roll and her voice squeaked: "Andrews, Gibbs, Hansen, Hawthorne, Hennessey, Matthews, Peters, Rocque, Welsch, Whitehead."

Everyone said "Here" dutifully.

"And now, children, we will have the election for officer. Are there any nominations?"

Sport leaped to his feet. "I nominate Harriet Welsch."

Janie yelled, "I second it." They always did this every year because the one that was officer controlled everything. When the teacher went out of the room the officer could write down the names of anyone who was disorderly. The officer also got to be the editor of the Sixth Grade Page in the school paper.

Rachel Hennessey got up. "I nominate Marion Hawthorne," she said in her prissiest voice.

Marion Hawthorne shot Beth Ellen Hansen a look that made Harriet's hair stand on end. Beth Ellen looked terrified, then got timidly to her feet and, almost whispering, managed to stammer, "I second it." It was rigged, the whole thing, every year. There were no more nominations and then came the vote. Marion Hawthorne got it. Every year either Marion or Rachel Hennessey got it. Harriet wrote in her book:

YOU'D THINK THE TEACHERS WOULD SMELL A RAT BECAUSE IT'S FIVE YEARS NOW AND NEITHER ME NOR SPORT NOR JANIE HAS EVER GOTTEN IT.

Marion Hawthorne looked terribly smug. Sport, Janie, and Harriet scowled at each other. Janie whispered, "Our day will come. Just wait." Harriet wondered if she meant that when she blew up the world Marion Hawthorne would see what they were made of. Or maybe Janie meant to blow up Marion Hawthorne first, which wasn't a bad idea.

It was finally three thirty-seven and school was over.

31

Sport came up to Harriet. "Hey, whyncha come over this afternoon?"

"After the spy route, maybe, if I've got time."

"Aw, gee, Janie's working in the lab. You both are always working."

"Why don't you practice? How're you ever going to be a ball player?"

"Can't. Have to clean the house. Come over if you get time."

Harriet said "okay," then "good-by," and ran toward the house. It was time for her cake and milk. Every day at three-forty she had cake and milk. Harriet loved doing everything every day in the same way.

"Time for my cake, for my cake and milk, time for my milk and cake." She ran yelling through the front door of her house. She ran through the front hall past the dining room and the living room and down the steps into the kitchen. There she ran smack into the cook.

"Like a missile you are, shot from that school," screamed the cook.

"Hello cook, hello, cooky, hello, hello, hello, hello," sang Harriet. Then she opened her notebook and wrote:

BLAH, BLAH, BLAH. I ALWAYS DO CARRY ON A LOT. ONCE OLE GOLLY SAID TO ME, "I COULD NEVER LOSE YOU IN A CROWD, I'D JUST FOLLOW THE SOUND OF YOUR VOICE."

She slammed the notebook and the cook jumped. Harriet laughed.

The cook put the cake and milk in front of her. "What you always writing in that dad-blamed book for?" she asked with a sour little face.

"Because," Harriet said around a bite of cake, "I'm a spy."

"Spy, huh. Some spy."

"I *am* a spy. I'm a *good* spy, too. I've never been caught."

Cook settled herself with a cup of coffee. "How long you been a spy?"

"Since I could write. Ole Golly told me if I was going to be a writer I better write down everything, so I'm a spy that writes down everything."

"Hmmmmmmph." Harriet knew the cook couldn't think of anything to say when she did that.

"I know all about you."

"Like fun, you do." The cook looked startled.

"I do too. I know you live with your sister in Brooklyn and that she might get married and you wish you had a car and you have a son that's no good and drinks."

"What do you do, child? Listen at doors?"

"Yes," said Harriet.

"Well, I never," said the cook. "I think that's bad manners."

"Ole Golly doesn't. Ole Golly says find out everything you can cause life is hard enough even if you know a lot."

"I bet she don't know you spooking round this house listening at doors."

"Well, how am I supposed to find out anything?"

"I don't know"—the cook shook her head—"I don't know about that Ole Golly."

"What do you mean?" Harriet felt apprehensive.

"I don't know. I just don't know. I wonder about her."

Ole Golly came into the room. "What is it you don't know?"

Cook looked as though she might hide under the table. She stood up. "Can I get you your tea, Miss Golly?" she asked meekly.

"That would be most kind of you," said Ole Golly and sat down.

Harriet opened her notebook:

I WONDER WHAT THAT WAS ALL ABOUT. MAYBE OLI
GOLLY KNOWS SOMETHING ABOUT COOK THAT COOK
DOESN'T WANT HER TO KNOW. CHECK ON THIS.

"What do you have in school this year, Harriet?"
asked Ole Golly.

"English, History, Geography, French, Math, ugh,
Science, ugh, and the Performing Arts, ugh, ugh, ugh."
Harriet rattled these off in a very bored way.

"What history?"

"Greeks and Romans, ugh, ugh, ugh."

"They're fascinating."

"What?"

"They are. Just wait, you'll see. Talk about spies.
Those gods spied on everybody all the time."

"Yeah?"

" 'Yes,' Harriet, not 'yeah.' "

"Well, *I* wish *I'd* never heard of them."

"Ah, there's a thought from Aesop for you: 'We
would often be sorry if our wishes were gratified.' "
Ole Golly gave a little moo of satisfaction after she
had delivered herself of this.

"I think I'll go now," Harriet said.

"Yes," said the cook, "go out and play."

Harriet stood up. "I do not go out to PLAY, I go
out to WORK!" and in as dignified a way as possible
she walked from the room and up the steps from the
kitchen. Then she began to run, and running furiously,
she went past the first floor with the living room and
dining room, the second floor with her parents' bedroom and the library, and on up to the third floor to her
little room and bath.

Harriet loved her room. It was small and cozy, and
the bathroom was a little one with a tiny window
which looked out over the park across the street. Her

34

room had a bigger window. She looked around, pleased as always by the order, the efficiency of it. She always picked up everything immediately, not because anyone nagged at her—no one ever had—but because it was her room and she liked to have it just so. Harriet was just so about a lot of things. Her room stood around her pleasantly, waiting for her. Her own small bed next to the window, her bookcase filled with her books, her toy box, which had been filled with toys but which now held her notebooks because it could be locked, her desk and chair at which she did her homework—all seemed to look back at her with affection. Harriet put her books down on the desk and hurriedly began to change into her spy clothes.

Her spy clothes consisted first of all of an ancient pair of blue jeans, so old that her mother had forbidden her to wear them, but which Harriet loved because she had fixed up the belt with hooks to carry her spy tools. Her tools were a flashlight, in case she were ever out at night, which she never was, a leather pouch for her notebook, another leather case for extra pens, a water canteen, and a boy scout knife which had, among other features, a screwdriver and a knife and fork which collapsed. She had never had occasion to eat anywhere, but someday it might come in handy.

She attached everything to the belt, and it all worked fine except that she rattled a little. Next she put on an old dark-blue sweatshirt with a hood which she wore at the beach house in the summer so that it still smelled of salt air in a comforting way. Then she put on an old pair of blue sneakers with holes over each of her little toes. Her mother had actually gone so far as to throw these out, but Harriet had rescued them from the garbage when the cook wasn't looking.

She finished by donning a pair of black-rimmed spectacles with no glass in them. She had found these once in her father's desk and now sometimes wore them even to school, because she thought they made her look smarter.

She stood back and looked at herself in the full-length mirror which hung on her bathroom door. She was very pleased. Then she ran quickly down the steps and out, banging the front door behind her.

CHAPTER 3

She was particularly excited as she ran along, because today she was adding a new spying place to her route. She had discovered a way into a private house around the corner. Private houses were much more difficult to get into than apartment buildings, and this was the first one Harriet had managed. It belonged to a Mrs. Agatha K. Plumber who was a very strange, rather theatrical lady who had once married a man of considerable means. She was now divorced, lived alone, and apparently talked on the telephone all day. Harriet had found this much out from first listening to several conversations between Mrs. Plumber's maid and an overly friendly garbage man. Harriet had pretended to play ball while the garbage was being picked up.

Just yesterday she had discovered that by timing it exactly she had just enough time to jump in the dumbwaiter and slide the door closed before the maid completed one of her frequent trips up and down the stairs. The dumbwaiter was no longer used but fortunately had not been boarded up. Since there was a small crack in the door, Harriet could see and hear perfectly.

She approached the house, looked through the kitchen windows, and saw the maid preparing a tray. She knew then that the next step would be to take the tray to the second floor. Not a moment to lose. The maid went into the pantry. Harriet stepped through the kitchen door and in one jump was in the dumbwaiter. She barely got the door slid down again before the maid was back in the room. The maid was humming "Miss Am-er-i-ker, look at her, Miss Am-er-i-ker" in a tuneless sort of way.

Then the tray was ready. The maid picked it up and left the room. Simultaneously Harriet started pulling on the ropes that hoisted the dumbwaiter. Terrified, she heard a lot of creaking. This would never do. Maybe she could bring some oil.

She arrived at the second floor. Her heart was beating so fast she was almost unable to breathe. She looked through the crack. The first thing she saw was a huge four-poster bed in the middle of which Mrs. Plumber sat, propped against immense pillows, telephone in hand, surrounded by magazines, books, candy boxes, and a litter of pink baby pillows.

"Well," Mrs. Plumber was saying decisively into the telephone, *"I have discovered the secret of life."*

Wow, thought Harriet.

"My dear, it's very simple, you just *take* to your *bed.* You just refuse to leave it for *anything* or *anybody.*"

Some secret, thought Harriet; that's the dumbest thing I ever heard of. Harriet hated bed anyway. In and out was her motto, and the less time there the better.

"Oh, yes, darling, I *know.* I *know* you *can't* run away from life, I *agree* with you. I *loathe* people that do that. But you see, I'm *not.* While I'm lying here I'm actually *working* because, you see, and this is the *divine* part, I'm *deciding* on a profession!"

You must be a hundred and two, thought Harriet; you better get going.

The maid came in with the tray. "Put it down there," said Mrs. Plumber rather crossly, then went back to the phone.

Harriet wrote in her notebook:

IT'S JUST WHAT OLE GOLLY SAYS. RICH PEOPLE ARE BORING. SHE SAYS WHEN PEOPLE DON'T DO ANYTHING THEY DON'T THINK ANYTHING, AND WHEN THEY DON'T THINK ANYTHING THERE'S NOTHING TO THINK ABOUT THEM. IF I HAD A DUMBWAITER I WOULD LOOK IN IT ALL THE TIME TO SEE IF ANYBODY WAS IN IT.

As though she were reading Harriet's mind, Mrs. Plumber said to the maid, "Did you hear a creak just now in that old dumbwaiter?"

"No, ma'am," said the maid.

"It was probably my imagination." She went back to the telephone. "My dear, I have *infinite* possibilities. Now don't you think I would make a *marv-e-lous* actress? Or there's *painting;* I could *paint.* What do you think of that? . . . Well, darling, I'm only *forty,* think of *Gauguin. . . .*"

Harriet started, very slowly, heart pounding, to pull the ropes that would start her downward. It had occurred to her that she'd better exit while Mrs. Plumber was blathering away or she would certainly be heard. There was a tiny creak as she got near the bottom, but she was fairly certain no one heard it. There, the main floor. She peeked into the kitchen. Empty. Could she make it? She scrambled down and ran for her life.

I have never run so fast, she thought as she careened around the corner. Panting, she sat on some steps and took out her book.

I THINK THIS MIGHT BE TOO DANGEROUS AN ASSIGNMENT. BUT I WOULD LIKE TO KNOW WHAT JOB SHE TAKES. BUT HOW CAN YOU WORK LYING DOWN? HOW DOES SHE PAY FOR ANYTHING JUST LYING THERE? I GUESS SHE JUST LIVES ON HER HUSBAND'S MONEY. DOES MY MOTHER MOOCH OFF MY FATHER? I'LL NEVER DO THAT. LOOK AT POOR SPORT. HE HAS TOO MUCH TO DO ALREADY WITHOUT ME LYING UP IN THE BED ALL DAY EATING.

Harriet had three more stops before she was finished for the day, but before she continued she decided to stop by and see Sport. On the way there she got thirsty and stopped in her favorite luncheonette for an egg cream. It was her favorite because it was there that she had first begun to hear what peculiar things people say to each other. She liked to sit at the counter with her egg cream and let the voices from the tables behind her float over her head. Several conversations were always going on at once. Sometimes she would play a game and not look at the people until from listening to them she had decided what they looked like. Then she would turn around and see if she were right.

"A chocolate egg cream, please."

"Certainly, Harriet. How are you?"

"Okay." Harriet sat down, pleased that she was known. She put her twelve cents down and sipped away as she listened.

"My father is a rat."

"So, I have to admit, I handled that case in a perfect way, a really perfect way. I said to the judge . . ."

"He's a rat because he thinks he's perfect."

"Listen, Jane, we have to go to Orchard Street and get that material. I can't live in that house one more minute without shades. Anyone could see in."

Harriet had to restrain herself at this point from looking around at a new possibility for the spy route. If *anyone* could see in . . .

"You know, I've lost very few cases in my time, even if I do say so."

"He's such a rat he never lets my mother open her trap."

Rat trap, thought Harriet.

"You have no idea what it's like to hide all the time. Geez, I can't even walk around in a slip."

Her egg cream finished, Harriet summed up her guesses. The boy with the rat father would be skinny, have black hair, and a lot of pimples. The lawyer who won all his cases would be short, puffy-looking, and be leaning forward. She got no picture of the shadeless girl but decided that she must be fat. She turned around.

At first she couldn't tell. Then she saw the boy with

42

black hair and pimples. She felt a surge of triumph. She looked at what must be the lawyer, one of two men. Then she listened to see if he were the one. No, the other one was the lawyer. He wasn't short and fat, he was long and thin, with a handsome face. She consoled herself with a faint puffiness he had around the eyes.

Well, no wonder she won't walk around in a slip, Harriet thought, looking at the girl with no shades; she's the fattest thing I ever saw.

Enough. Only two out of three. Some days were better than others. She slid off the stool and went on her way to Sport's house. Sport lived in an apartment that was up four flights of stairs. He opened the door, wearing an apron and carrying a dishtowel. "Hi, Harriet, come in, I just got to do these dishes."

"Then whataya gonna do?"

"Then I sweep."

"Aw, Sport, you got too much work to do."

"Yeah, but what can I do? Somebody's got to do it. Once I didn't do it, and after a week I couldn't find the living room."

They went into the kitchen and Sport continued to do the dishes. Harriet pointed toward a closed door to the right of the kitchen. "Is *he* in there?"

"Yeah, he worked all night, so he's sleeping. I got to go to the store and then get back in time to fix his dinner."

"I couldn't even *fix* dinner, much less for my father. How do you do it?"

"Well, lots of times, you know, it's Eggsville."

"Doesn't he care what he eats?"

"Writers don't care what they eat. They just care what you think of them. Here, Harriet, hold this."

"I sure care what *I* eat." Just as she was saying this, Harriet heard a loud groan from the bedroom. She almost dropped the plate. "Hey, what's that?"

43

Sport looked totally unconcerned. "Nothing, just a bad dream. He has them all the time. Writers have a lot of bad dreams."

"Don't you want to be a writer, Sport? Gee, your father could even help you."

Sport almost collapsed at the sink. "Are you kidding? You *know* I want to be a ball player. And if I'm not a *good* ball player, I'll tell you something, I'm going to be a C.P.A."

"What's *that?*"

"You don't know what a C.P.A. is?" Sport screeched.

"No," said Harriet. She never minded admitting she didn't know something. So what, she thought; I could always learn.

"Well, I'll show you what that is. Come with me." Sport put the dishtowel down, took Harriet by the hand, and led her into his room. You would have known it was Sport's room because it was as neat as a pin. There was a little cot, made up army fashion, one straight chair, and a little desk. The desk was absolutely bare. Sport took a ring of keys out of his pocket and started unlocking the drawers to the desk. "You see these books? These are my books." He stepped back proudly. Harriet looked. Each drawer was filled with large ledgers. One drawer held a cashbox, which was also locked.

"My, my," she said, because she didn't know what else to say.

"A C.P.A. is an accountant, for your information," Sport said pompously, pulling back Harriet's hand sharply because she had started to reach for one of the ledgers.

"What's in all those?" asked Harriet, suspecting that they were empty.

"Our FINANCES. What do you think?" Sport was getting irritated.

"I hate money," Harriet said.

44

"Well, you'd jolly well like it if you didn't have any," Sport said arrogantly. Harriet considered this. It was true. She'd never had to think about it.

"Well, gee, Sport, do you like to do that? Isn't it just a lot of math?"

"Well, the math isn't hard; that's not it. I can't explain. Don't you know what I mean? Then you know where everything *is*."

"Oh," said Harriet, who did not understand at all.

"I mean, see, my father gets a check, and if I don't take it, then the next day it's gone and he just throws up his hands and goes in his room and shuts the door. Then we don't eat."

"Really?"

"Really. This way I take the check and I cash it and I plan what to do with all the money piece by piece and then we have enough to eat. See?"

"Yeah. That's very sensible."

"Well, I don't know what would have happened to us if I hadn't started doing that."

"Yeah. Gee, I never knew this about you, Sport."

Sport kind of kicked a foot around on the floor. Then they both felt embarrassed, so Sport went back into the kitchen, and Harriet, in the living room, seized this opportunity to try to see through the keyhole into Sport's father's room. She saw nothing but an old gym sock lying on the floor. Sport came into the living room and Harriet jumped back, then said quickly, "Well, I got to get back to my spy route. I'll see you tomorrow."

"Okay, I'll see ya," said Sport as he opened the door for her.

When the door closed behind her Harriet stood a minute thinking. Then she ran down the steps. When she got outside, she sat on the steps and wrote in her notebook:

SPORT'S HOUSE SMELLS LIKE OLD LAUNDRY, AND IT'S

NOISY AND KIND OF POOR-LOOKING. MY HOUSE DOESN'T
SMELL AND IS QUIET LIKE MRS. PLUMBER'S. DOES THAT
MEAN WE ARE RICH? WHAT MAKES PEOPLE POOR OR
RICH?

She walked along a little way, then was suddenly
struck by another idea.

ARE RICH PEOPLE EVER GOING TO GROW UP TO BE
WRITERS OR ARE WRITERS ALL LIKE MR. ROCQUE WITH
NO MONEY? MY FATHER IS ALWAYS SAYING STARVING-
ARTIST OR STARVINGWRITER. MAYBE I BETTER REDUCE.

Harriet headed toward the Dei Santis' grocery, the
first stop on her regular spy route. The grocery was on
York Avenue, and there was a little alleyway beside
it that provided three vantage points from which Harriet could watch. One was a window facing the alley,
affording a view of the rear of the counter at which
Papa Dei Santi stood. The other window on the alley
showed the back of the store with the table around
which the family ate lunch. The third window was
around the back, in the courtyard, and showed the
storeroom where Little Joe Curry worked all day.

She crept into the alley. Nothing was doing at the
first window. She kept her body low and scooted to
the second window. Suddenly she saw the whole family. She had to duck her head quickly in order not to
be seen. Luckily the window was open a fraction, so
she could hear what was being said.

Mama Dei Santi was speaking, *"Accidente!!* He take
the truck, get killed!"

Harriet knew she must be talking about Fabio.
Fabio was always wanting to take the truck somewhere. She peeked over the sill.

Fabio leaned against a packing case. A cigarette
dangled from his mouth. He was tall, very thin, and

had a gloomy look. He shifted slightly in irritation at his mother's remark.

His mother caught his mood and raised both hands high above her head. "What did I do to God to deserve to come to a country like this that should come down on my head to raise a son like you?"

"Oh, Mama." That was Maria Elena. She looked in the mirror all day and said dumb things. She was seventeen and very beautiful.

"Don't you Mama me. Look at Bruno, all day, all night, work in the store. *That's* a son." Mama Dei Santi spewed forth these words in a hiss.

Harriet peeked over the sill. Franca, who was fourteen and a complete blank of a person, leaned against the wall as though she had been propped there. Dino, who was six, traveled a toy car with his hand along one of the shelves. Papa Dei Santi turned slowly to Fabio. *"Mio figlio,"* he began in a tired patient voice, "I work my life away for you. I come here with nothing. I get a pushcart. I sell vegetables. You know what makes a man that sells vegetables?"

Fabio frowned. The cigarette hardly moved in his mouth as he spoke. "You now *got* the store, Papa. You now got the truck. Can I borrow the truck?"

"No *good*. No *good*," Papa Dei Santi screamed with all his might.

There was a moment of strange silence as Fabio and his father stood staring at each other. Bruno walked heavily into the room. He was a thick, strong man with thick, strong thoughts in his head. He spoke slowly as though the thoughts had to come from a long way back in his head. "Let him take the car, Papa. Let him have a little fun. He's eighteen. He just wants a little fun."

"Fun, fun. Eighteen too old for fun. What fun you have, Bruno?"

"We're different, Papa. Let him go. You make him bad if you stop him."

"Bad? *Bad?* He's already bad. Flunk out the school. Hang around, lazy bum, all day. How I *make* him bad?"

"Oh, Papa," Maria Elena breathed softly as she leaned toward the mirror.

"Buzz, buzz, buzz," Dino whispered, having turned the car into an airplane.

The bell on the door of the shop rang, breaking into their anguish. Papa Dei Santi started toward the front. "Customer," he said under his breath, "no more talk. Everybody to work."

"Papa." It was only one word, but it took Fabio an enormous effort to get it out.

"No truck." Papa Dei Santi didn't even turn around. The words came out like bullets.

Fabio slumped, took a long drag on the cigarette without putting his hand to it. Maria Elena tried her hair a new way in the mirror. Mama Dei Santi walked heavily toward the front, following Bruno. No one looked at Fabio. Harriet squatted under the window and wrote out everything she had seen. Then she wrote:

THAT FABIO MAY BE BAD BUT I DON'T BLAME HIM. I WOULDN'T WANT TO BE LIKE BRUNO EITHER. BRUNO LOOKS LIKE A BIG DUMB BEAR.

ONCE I THOUGHT I WANTED TO BE FRANCA AND LIVE IN THAT FAMILY. BUT SHE'S SO DULL IF I WAS HER I COULDN'T STAND MYSELF. I GUESS IT'S NOT MONEY THAT MAKES PEOPLE DULL. THERE IS A LOT I DON'T KNOW ABOUT THIS THING OF BEING DULL. I BETTER FIND OUT BECAUSE I MIGHT BE IT.

WHAT IS IT LIKE TO HAVE BROTHERS AND SISTERS?

ONE THING, WHENEVER THEY YELLED IT WOULDN'T
ALWAYS BE AT YOU. SOMETIMES IT WOULD BE AT YOUR
BROTHER THEN YOU COULD LAUGH.

WHAT IS TOO OLD TO HAVE FUN? YOU CAN'T BE TOO
OLD TO SPY EXCEPT IF YOU WERE FIFTY YOU MIGHT
FALL OFF A FIRE ESCAPE, BUT YOU COULD SPY AROUND
ON THE GROUND A LOT.

Harriet closed her book and crept around the back
to see what Little Joe Curry was doing. Little Joe Curry
was the delivery boy for the Dei Santis and he was always up to one thing. He was always eating. It was
strange the Dei Santis made any money at all the way
Little Joe ate.

Harriet peeked in. He was sitting there now, when
he should have been working, eating a pound of
cheese. Next to him, waiting to be consumed, sat two
cucumbers, three tomatoes, a loaf of bread, a custard
pie, three quarts of milk, a meatball sandwich about
two feet long, two jars—one of pickles, one of mayonnaise—four apples, and a large salami. Harriet's eyes
widened and she wrote:

WHEN I LOOK AT HIM I COULD EAT A THOUSAND TOMATO
SANDWICHES.

Harriet heard a little whispering noise in the alley.
She knew who it was without even looking, because
she was almost caught every day by the same people.
Four skinny little kids appeared around the side of
the house. They tiptoed up to the door and knocked
discreetly. They were very poor children with torn
dirty clothes and smudges all over their faces as though
they were never washed. The oldest was around seven
and the others were around four and five.

Little Joe opened the door. There wasn't a word ex-

changed as he handed them a tomato, a quart of milk, half of the cheese, the loaf of bread, half the salami, half the custard pie, and two apples. They distributed these things among themselves to make for easy carrying and scooted away down the alley as silently as they had come.

Little Joe went back to his eating. Harriet felt funny watching the scene. She sighed a little, then creeping along under the windows, went on to her next stop.

That night as Harriet lay in her bathtub taking her bath before dinner she felt very happy. She had done a good day's work. She listened to Ole Golly, who was going through Harriet's closet taking out things that needed cleaning. Ole Golly was whistling. It was a cheery though tuneless sort of whistling which Harriet rather liked. The yellow paint on the tiny bathroom walls looked clean and happy. Harriet felt warm and sleepy in the hot water.

Suddenly the front door banged downstairs and Harriet could hear her father's voice.

"Finks, finks, double-barreled rat, rat, rat, finks, finks, finks." He sounded very angry. Harriet could tell from his voice that he had stormed up the steps to the library. "You won't *believe* the iniquity . . . you will *not believe* when I tell you the unmitigated *finkiness* of those guys."

Then Mrs. Welsch's voice, calm and comforting, obviously leading him to a chair. "What, darling? My heavens, what is it?"

"Well, mumble mumble, they're just the worst mumble mumble. I just *could not believe . . .*"

"Darling, here, have your drink."

Harriet was standing up in the bathtub, she was trying so hard to hear.

"What did you do today, Harriet?"

How annoying. Ole Golly had chosen *this* time to

start a conversation. Harriet pretended not to hear as she kept listening.

"That mumble, he's an absolutely *inspired* fink, that's what he is, a real mumble I tell you, I never saw a mumble like him."

"Did you take a lot of notes?" Harriet tried to crane her ears past Ole Golly's question. Would she *just* shut up a minute?

"Darling, that's terrible, simply mumble."

"I don't know what I'm going to do. They're really going to mumble it up. If anything it'll be the worst show of the season. They're real mumbles, they are."

"What are you doing, Harriet M. Welsch, standing up in that bathtub?" Ole Golly looked exceedingly fierce. "Sit down there this minute and I'll wash your back. Look at those ears. Do you perhaps *pour* ink into them?"

"No, they itch a lot."

"That doesn't mean a thing, all that noise downstairs."

"Well, I'd like to hear it all the same."

"Your father has a very high-pressure job, that's all."

"What's a high-pressure job?"

"It means he's not allowed to do exactly what he wants with the job, and what he is allowed to do he isn't given enough time to do it in."

"Oh," said Harriet, thinking, What does *that* mean? "Do spies have high pressure?"

"Oh, yes, if they get caught."

"I'm never caught."

"Not yet."

"Ole Golly, are you ever going away?"

"When you get so big you don't need me, yes, but not right this minute. You're getting pretty old though," Ole Golly said, surveying Harriet critically.

There was a pause, then Harriet said, "Ole Golly, do you have a boy friend?"

"Yes," said Ole Golly and looked away.

"*YES!*" Harriet almost fainted into her bath water.

"Yes," said Ole Golly with dignity. "Now time for dinner."

There was a pause and then Harriet asked, "It's unsanitary to have a lot of cats in the house, isn't it?"

Ole Golly looked rather startled. "I always think of cats as rather clean, but then, a *lot* of cats . . . How many cats?"

"I think twenty-five, but I'm not sure. They move around a lot."

"*Twenty-five?* Here's your towel. Who do you know with twenty-five cats?"

"Oh, somebody." Harriet adored being mysterious.

"Who?"

"Oh, just somebody." And Harriet smiled to herself.

Ole Golly knew better than to pursue it. She always said that privacy was very important, especially to spies.

When Harriet was all through with her dinner and bundled off to bed, she began to think of Harrison Withers and all his cats. Harrison Withers lived on Eighty-second at the top of a dilapidated rooming house. He had two rooms, one for him and one for the cats. In his room he had a bed, a chair, a work table at which he made birdcages, and a whole wall of birdcage-making tools. In the other room there was nothing but the cats. In the kitchen there was one glass, one cup, and twenty-six plates all stacked up.

It suddenly occurred to Harriet to wonder if he ate exactly the same food as the cats, or different food. She must find out tomorrow. She could find out by following him around the supermarket. She fell asleep contentedly. Right before she fell asleep she wondered who in the world Ole Golly's boy friend was.

CHAPTER 4

The next afternoon, after her cake and milk, Harriet went straight to Mrs. Plumber's house. She knew it was dangerous, but once her curiosity was aroused she had never been able to give up a spot on her route. As she got to the house she saw Little Joe Curry in conversation with the maid. She sidled around the front, took a ball from her pocket that she always carried for such moments, and began to engage in an innocent-looking game of ball right in front of them.

Little Joe was leaning against the door. He always looked tired when he wasn't eating. The maid sounded very aggravated. "Haven't got the change. She went off left me without a cent."

"Well, when will she be back? I could come back."

"Lord knows. When she go to Elizabeth Arden she sometimes gone all day. Lot of work to do on her, you know." The maid giggled nastily.

"Man, she got all that jack and don't pay. They all alike—more they got, less they pay." And with that pronouncement Little Joe shuffled off back for his afternoon snack.

Harriet looked unconcerned as he went past. The

maid went inside. Harriet leaned against the hydrant and wrote:

I WONDER WHAT THEY DO TO HER ALL DAY. I ONCE SAW MY MOTHER IN A MUD PACK. THEY'LL NEVER GET ME IN A MUD PACK.

She slammed her book and went to the Dei Santis'. The store was terribly busy. Everyone was running to and fro, even Franca who usually had to be propped up somewhere. Little Joe wasn't even back yet. Well, thought Harriet, this looks like a rotten spy day. She checked Mrs. Plumber and the Dei Santis off her list and went on to the Robinsons, the next people on the route.

The Robinsons were a couple who lived in a duplex on Eighty-eighth Street. When they were alone they never said a word to each other. Harriet liked to watch them when they had company, because it made her laugh to see them showing off their house. Because the Robinsons had only one problem. They thought they were perfect.

Luckily their living room was on the ground floor of their duplex. Harriet scurried through the back passageway to the garden and there, by leaning around a box kept for garden tools, she could see in without being seen.

The Robinsons were sitting, as they always were, staring into space. They never worked, and what was worse, they never even read anything. They bought things and brought them home and then they had people in to look at them. Otherwise they didn't seem to do a blessed thing.

The doorbell rang.

"Ah," said Mrs. Robinson. "There they are now."

She got up sedately and walked slowly, even though she had obviously been sitting there waiting for the

ring. She looked critically as Mr. Robinson adjusted his smoking jacket, then went to the door.

"Come in, Jack, Martha, how lovely to see you. It's been so long. How long will you be in town?"

"Well, we—"

"Look, before you go a step further, look, Martha, at these lovely vinyl squares I just got put in. Aren't they just perfect?"

"Yes, they are—"

"And that chest in the corner, isn't that a find?"

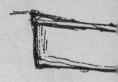

"Well, it's just . . ."

Mr. Robinson stood up. "Hello there, Jack."

"Hi there, fella. Long time no—"

"Hey, Jack, I wanta show you my gun collection. You haven't been here since I got two new ones. Just come in here and . . ." They disappeared from Harriet's view.

"Martha, come here. You must see the . . . oh, here, put your coat and purse down in this perfect place, this eighteenth-century luggage rack. Isn't it divine?"

"Why, yes, it's—"

"Look, come here, right over here, now *isn't* that the most beautiful garden you've ever seen?"

"Yes, oooh, aaah, it's just—"

"You know, Martha, we have the most perfect life. . . ."

"You don't have any children, do you, Grace?"

"Why, no, but frankly we think that's just perfect. . . ."

Harriet, having ducked when they looked at the garden, fell over laughing. When she recovered herself she grabbed her notebook.

BOY, OLE GOLLY TOLD ME ONCE THAT SOME PEOPLE THINK THEY'RE PERFECT BUT SHE OUGHTA SEE THESE TWO. IF THEY HAD A BABY IT WOULD LAUGH IN ITS

HEAD ALL THE TIME AT THEM SO IT'S A GOOD THING
THEY DON'T. ALSO IT MIGHT NOT BE PERFECT. THEN
THEY MIGHT KILL IT. I'M GLAD I'M NOT PERFECT—I'D
BE BORED TO DEATH. BESIDES IF THEY'RE SO GREAT WHY
DO THEY JUST SIT THERE ALL DAY STARING AT NOTHING?
THEY COULD BE CRAZY AND NOT EVEN KNOW IT.

She headed over to Harrison Withers' house. She
liked to look at the birdcages he made but, more than
that, she intended to be there when he got caught. The
Health Department was forever trying to get in to catch
him because he had too many cats, but Harrison
Withers was very crafty. Whenever his doorbell rang
he looked out the window, and if the man ringing the
bell wore a hat, he never let him in. All the men in the
Health Department wore hats and Harrison Withers
didn't know anybody who wore a hat.

Harriet climbed the steps to the top floor of his
rooming house and the last flight that led up to the
roof. She could look through one skylight at a place
where the paint had been worn away, and she was
sure she couldn't be seen from inside.

She peered down. As she did, she remembered that
she had planned to watch him in the supermarket to
see if he lived on kidneys like the cats.

The cats were all milling around. She went to the

other skylight. Sunlight flooded the other room but here caught glints from tools, from the tiny shining minarets which topped the cages. Harriet liked to look at this room. The cages were beautiful soaring things, and when he was in this room, Harrison Withers was a happy man.

Harriet liked to watch him work, admired the patience which allowed him to sit bent over for hours twisting minuscule wires around ridiculously small connections.

Oh, what luck! Harrison Withers was just coming through the door with a big shopping bag. Now she could see what he ate. The cats all followed him into the kitchen as he started taking things out of the bag. They started mewing and rubbing against his legs as he took kidney after kidney out of the bag.

"There now, children," he spoke to them gently. He always spoke very softly. "There now. We're all going to eat now. Hello, everybody—yes, yes, hello. Hello, David, hello, Rasputin, yes, Goethe, Alex, Sandra, Thomas Wolfe, Pat, Puck, Faulkner, Cassandra, Gloria, Circe, Koufax, Marijane, Willy Mays, Francis, Kokoschka, Donna, Fred, Swann, Mickey Mantle, Sebastian, Yvonne, Jerusalem, Dostoievsky, and Barnaby. Hello, hello, hello."

Harriet had counted this time. There were twenty-six. Then that meant that the twenty-six plates were for the cats. What did he eat from? She watched as he pulled from the very bottom of the bag one small container of yogurt. Cats don't eat yogurt, thought Harriet; that must be what he eats.

She watched while he fed the cats then spooned a bit of yogurt into his mouth. He went into his workroom, carrying the container, and closed the door behind him because the cats were not allowed in that room. He sat at his work table before a particularly beautiful cage, a replica of a Victorian summer house.

Quiet descended upon the room as he sat studying the cage. His hand moved as in a dream to put the yogurt to one side. He looked lovingly, his eyes slightly glazed, at the one small unfinished portion of the structure. Very slowly he moved one piece a quarter of an inch to the left. He sat back and looked at it a long time. Then he moved it back.

Harriet wrote in her notebook:

HE LOVES TO DO THAT. IS THIS WHAT OLE GOLLY MEANS? SHE SAYS PEOPLE WHO LOVE THEIR WORK LOVE LIFE. DO SOME PEOPLE HATE LIFE? ANYWAY I WOULDN'T MIND LIVING LIKE HARRISON WITHERS BECAUSE HE

LOOKS HAPPY EXCEPT I WOULDN'T LIKE <u>ALL</u> THOSE
CATS. I MIGHT EVEN LIKE A DOG.

She took one last look at Harrison Withers, who was
gently winding a piece of wire around two little curling pieces of wood. She got up then and went down to
the street. In front of the house she stopped to write:

THERE IS ALSO THAT YOGURT. THINK OF EATING THAT
ALL THE TIME. THERE IS NOTHING LIKE A GOOD TOMATO
SANDWICH NOW AND THEN.

She decided to go see Janie awhile before going on
to the rest of her route. Janie lived in the garden
duplex of a renovated brownstone off East End Avenue on Eighty-fourth Street. Harriet rang the outside
bell and pushed the door when it buzzed back. Janie
was standing inside at her doorway and she was in a
foul mood. Harriet could tell just by looking at her.
Janie always looked terribly cheerful when she was in
her most angry mood. Harriet figured it had to be that
way because Janie's normal face was one of sheer
rage. Today she smiled happily and sang out winning-
ly, "Hello, there, Harriet Welsch." Things couldn't be
worse.

Harriet walked toward her tentatively, as one would
toward a mad dog, trying to see Janie's eyes more
clearly, but Janie whipped inside the door. Harriet
followed her in.

"What's the matter?" Harriet whispered. They were
standing in the little foyer off the living room.

"They're after me," whispered Janie, still smiling
wildly.

"Who?"

"The Rat Pack." This was what Janie called her
mother, her father, her brother, and her grandmother
who lived with them.

"Why?"

"My mother says I'm going to blow us all up and that I have to go to dancing school. Come past here, then they won't see us." Janie was hissing through her outrageous smile as she led them up the back steps to what she called her lab but which was really her room.

One corner of her room had been stripped bare. The rug had been pulled back, exposing one corner where Janie had started to cut off the excess to get it out of the way, but which she had been stopped from doing by her mother in an hysterical fit. At that time there had been a large fight through which Janie grinned broadly, and her mother let her know that it didn't make a whit of difference if they didn't ordinarily have rugs in labs ("They catch fire," Janie had said, which had set her mother off again), that Janie had a rug in her room that was going to stay there, and that the very best she could hope for was to have it rolled back. So it lay there in a roll at the end of the room.

The lab itself was very complex and frightened Harriet whenever she looked at it, although she never would have admitted this to Janie. It consisted of rows and rows of shelves filled with bottles, all filled with suspicious fluids and looking as though you would turn into Mr. Hyde if you drank them. Only Janie understood anything whatever about them, and she wouldn't explain but instead called everyone a cretin who asked her. The maids wouldn't go near Janie's room, so years ago she had had to learn to clean it herself.

Harriet stood staring at all the equipment while Janie rushed over to something boiling furiously on a Bunsen burner. She fiddled with it and turned it lower, then turned back to Harriet. "This time I may really get it," she said thoughtfully and went over and flopped on her bed.

"You mean . . ."

"Yes. They may take it *all* away."

"Oh, they couldn't."

"There have been people before me who have been misunderstood. They could." And the way Janie said this, with her smile dropped and her eyes boring into Harriet's, made shivers run up Harriet's back.

"What would you do?"

"Leave. Of course." One thing about Janie, thought Harriet, she never has a moment's hesitation about anything.

"What is this about dancing school?"

"Just wait, buddy. They're going to get you too. I heard my mother talking to your mother. Who ever heard of Pasteur going to dancing school? Or Madame Curie or Einstein?" Janie spit out the names.

Harriet couldn't think of any spies who went to dancing school either. This was a bad development. "Whether they know it or not, I'm not going," Harriet said firmly.

"They will *never get me*," Janie said very loudly. Then in a different tone, "Hey, Harriet, I've got to finish this experiment."

"That's all right. I've got some things to put in my notebook. Go ahead." Janie got up briskly and went over to her lab table. "If I don't do it now, this thing will curdle."

"What are you making?"

There was no answer. There was never any answer when you asked Janie this, but Harriet did it every now and then just to be polite. It was something explosive. That much was perfectly clear. Harriet sat looking around her for a while, at Janie's back bent attentively over her work, at the sunlight coming in the window—the late afternoon sun which looked sad and pleasant at the same time and which reminded her abruptly of New Year's Day last year. There

hadn't been anything important about that day. She
had just happened to look at the sun in the same way.
She leaned back on the bed. It would be nice to be
here or somewhere like this every day.

MAYBE WHEN I GROW UP I CAN HAVE AN OFFICE. ON THE
DOOR IT CAN SAY "HARRIET THE SPY" IN GOLD LETTERS.
AND THEN IT CAN HAVE OFFICE HOURS LIKE THE DEN-

TIST'S DOOR HAS AND UNDERNEATH IT CAN SAY <u>ANY SPY</u> <u>WORK UNDERTAKEN.</u> I GUESS I WON'T PUT THE PRICE ON THE DOOR. THEN THEY'LL HAVE TO COME IN AND ASK ME. I CAN GO THERE EVERY DAY FROM ELEVEN TO FOUR AND WRITE IN MY NOTEBOOK. PEOPLE WILL COME IN AND TELL ME WHO TO GO AND SPY ON AND I CAN DO THAT OUTSIDE OF OFFICE HOURS. I WONDER IF I WILL GET ANY MURDER CASES. I WOULD HAVE TO HAVE A GUN AND FOLLOW PEOPLE BUT I BET IT WOULD BE AT NIGHT AND I WOULDN'T BE ALLOWED OUT.

"Hey, Janie, if you were going to slit somebody's throat, wouldn't you do it in the dead of night?"

"I'd poison them." Janie didn't even turn around.

I bet you would, thought Harriet. "But, Janie, they'd just trace the poison."

"Not the one I've got."

"Did you make a new one?"

"Yes."

Harriet went back to her notebook.

WELL, MAYBE THERE'S SOMETHING TO THIS CHEMISTRY AFTER ALL. I COULD POISON PINKY AND NO ONE WOULD EVER KNOW IT. I BET THEY NEED SOME NEW POISONS. BUT OLE GOLLY SAYS THAT IN WASHINGTON THEY'VE ALREADY GOT A LITTLE TUBE WITH A SPOONFUL OF SOMETHING IN IT THAT WILL BLOW UP THE WHOLE WORLD, MAYBE THE WHOLE UNIVERSE. WHAT WOULD HAPPEN? WOULD WE FLY THROUGH THE AIR? IN SPACE YOU JUST FLOAT AROUND. I WOULD BE LONELY.

"Oh, *boy*, is that maddening," Janie stormed away from the lab table and sat down with her arms folded.

"What happened?" Harriet looked up.

"I goofed," Janie said. "If I'd done it right, it would have made a terrific noise."

"What would your mother have done?"

"That's who the noise was for, silly. If they think I'll set foot in a dancing school, they're off their rockers."

"Why don't you blow up the dancing school?" Harriet asked sensibly.

"Oh, they'd just find another place to have it. I know this kind of thing. Once they get this kind of thing in their heads, forget it. The only way out is to absolutely refuse. My mother hates to spend money, that's one thing; so if she can make a joke out of my not wanting to, then I'm in the clear because then she can save the money."

Harriet knew what she meant. Mrs. Gibbs tried to make a bad joke out of everything. Mrs. Welsch always spoke of Janie's mother as "that smart nose, Mabel Gibbs." Harriet thought to herself that one thing she couldn't stand was the kind of person who thought she was funny when she wasn't.

"See, if she can get across to her friends the idea that I'm an impossible eccentric, then it won't be her fault I'm not in dancing school," Janie went on. "And as for me, I couldn't care less if I learn to dance. I've got a big picture of Newton learning the Charleston."

Janie had a definite mind. That was one thing you could say for her. Harriet admired it.

There was a knock on the door. "Oh, brother," Janie said and got up to answer it.

It was Janie's mother. She gave her big horse laugh as she came into the room. "Well, well, how's Dr. Caligari?" she boomed out and laughed again raucously.

It's a good thing *she* laughs, thought Harriet, because no one else ever does. Janie looked at her mother stony-faced. Harriet did the same.

"That's my kid, a bundle of fun," and so saying Mrs. Gibbs slapped Janie on the back with such a wallop that Janie almost fell to the floor. Recovering herself, she glared again, a hideous smile beginning to creep across her face.

" 'Yes, sir, that's my baby. No, sir, don't mean maybe,' " Mrs. Gibbs began to sing in her rollicking way while Harriet and Janie looked at the floor in a state of acute embarrassment. Noticing finally that she had no audience, Mrs. Gibbs stopped. "Well, Harriet," she hollered, "haven't seen you in a long time. Have a nice summer?" Mrs. Gibbs never waited for an answer from children, thinking they were too shy to speak (which they always were around her), but zoomed on with her shouts. "Talked to your mother the other day. Has Janie told you about dancing school? Your mother's all for it and I am too. You girls need a few graces, you know, turning into young women any day now, don't want to be clumps on the dance floor, nothing more embarrassing than a wallflower. Your mother's worried about the way you move, Harriet." And she suddenly focused on Harriet, waking her out of a reverie.

"Fast," Harriet said, "that's the way I move, fast. What's wrong with that?"

Mrs. Gibbs stared at her. Janie went back to her lab table. Mrs. Gibbs, not having any idea how to take Harriet's comment, decided, as she always did, that the best thing was to laugh it off. She gave an enormous whoop of laughter. Harriet saw Janie's shoulders go up in a quick little embarrassed cringe.

"Well, now, aren't you something. Wait'll I tell Harry that. You're as bad as Janie." She laughed a lot more for good measure. "Well, we'll just see about that. I think you girls have something to learn. I think you have to find out you're girls. I think we might just get together, all us mothers, and blast a little sense into your heads"—her hand was on the doorknob—"and I don't mean *your* kind of blast, Dr. Jekyll." She started to open the door and at that moment there was a terrific noise. Something on the lab table flew straight up into the air, and Mrs. Gibbs went through the door like a shot.

Janie turned around and they both looked at the door through which came several different screams and feet clattering as Mrs. Gibbs tore down the steps, screeching, "Harry Gibbs, she's done it. Harry, come here, Harry, that maniac will kill us all, Harry Gibbs, come here, she's blown up the house!"

They listened to a whispered colloquy in the downstairs hall after Harry had run out, saying, "WHAT! WHAT? What's happened?"

After the whispers there was an ominous silence during which they must have realized that the house was still standing. Then Harry's voice—"I'll go speak to her"—and his feet beginning the climb.

Harriet had no desire to watch Mr. Gibbs's tiny perspiring face as he tried to cope with his daughter. It would only make it worse for him if she was there.

"I think I'll just go down the back steps," she said gently, going toward the door.

"I guess you better." Janie sounded tired.

"Don't give up," Harriet whispered as she left.

"Never," Janie whispered back.

CHAPTER 5

That night at dinner everything was going along as usual, that is, Mr. and Mrs. Welsch were having an interminable, rambling conversation about nothing in particular while Harriet watched it all like a tennis match, when suddenly Harriet leaped to her feet as though she had just then remembered, and screamed, "I'll be *damned* if I'll go to dancing school."

"Harriet!" Mrs. Welsch was appalled. "How dare you use words like that at the table."

"Or any other place, dear," interjected Mr. Welsch calmly.

"All right, I'll be FINKED if I'll go to dancing school." Harriet stood and screamed this solidly. She was throwing a fit. She only threw fits as a last resort, so that even as she did it she had a tiny feeling in the back of her brain that she had already lost. She wouldn't, however, have it said that she went down without a try.

"Where in the world did you learn a word like that?" Mrs. Welsch's eyebrows were raised almost to her hairline.

"It's not a verb, anyway," said Mr. Welsch. They

70

both sat looking at Harriet as though she were a curiosity put on television to entertain them.

"I *will not,* I *will not,* I *will not,*" shouted Harriet at the top of her lungs. She wasn't getting the right reaction. Something was wrong.

"Oh, but you will," said Mrs. Welsch calmly. "It really isn't so bad. You don't even know what it's like."

"I hated it," said Mr. Welsch and went back to his dinner.

"I *do so* know what's it's like." Harriet was getting tired of standing up and screaming. She wished she could sit down but it wouldn't have done. It would have looked like giving up. "I went there once on a visit with Beth Ellen because she had to go and I was spending the night, and you have to wear party dresses and all the boys are too short and you feel like a *hippopotamus.*" She said this all in one breath and screamed "hippopotamus."

Mr. Welsch laughed. "An accurate description, you must admit."

"Darling, the boys get taller as you go along."

"I just *won't.*" Somehow, indefinably, Harriet felt she was losing ground all the time.

"It isn't so bad." Mrs. Welsch went back to her dinner.

This was too much. The point wasn't coming across at all. They had to be roused out of their complacency. Harriet took a deep breath, and in as loud a voice as she could, repeated, "I'll be *damned* if I'll go!"

"All right, that does it." Mrs. Welsch stood up. She was furious. "You're getting your mouth washed out with soap, young lady. Miss Golly, Miss Golly, step in here a minute." When there was no response, Mrs. Welsch rang the little silver dinner bell and in a moment Cook appeared.

Harriet stood petrified. *Soap!*

"Cook, will you tell Miss Golly to step in here a minute." Mrs. Welsch stood looking at Harriet as though she were a worm, as Cook departed. "Now, Harriet, to your room. Miss Golly will be up shortly."

"But . . ."

"Your *room*," said Mrs. Welsch firmly, pointing to the door.

Feeling rather like an idiot, Harriet left the dining room. She thought for half a second about waiting around and listening outside but decided it was too risky.

She went up to her room and waited. Ole Golly came in a few minutes later.

"Well, now, what is this about dancing school?" she asked amiably.

"I'm not going," Harriet said meekly. There was something that made her feel ridiculous when she shouted at Ole Golly. Maybe because she never got the feeling with Ole Golly that she did with her parents that they never heard anything.

"Why not?" Ole Golly asked sensibly.

Harriet thought a minute. The other reasons weren't really it. It was that the thought of being in dancing school somehow made her feel undignified. Finally she had it. *"Spies* don't go to dancing school," she said triumphantly.

"Oh, but they do," said Ole Golly.

"They do *not*," said Harriet rudely.

"Harriet"—Ole Golly took a deep breath and sat down—"have you ever thought about how spies are trained?"

"Yes. They learn languages and guerrilla fighting and everything about a country so if they're captured they'll know all the old football scores and things like that."

"That's *boy* spies, Harriet. You're not thinking."

Harriet hated more than anything else to be told

72

by Ole Golly that she wasn't thinking. It was worse than any soap. "What do you mean?" she asked quietly.

"What about *girl* spies? What are they taught?"

"The same things."

"The same things and a few more. Remember that movie we saw about Mata Hari one night on television?"

"Yes . . ."

"Well, think about that. Where did she operate? Not in the woods guerrilla fighting, right? She went to parties, right? And remember that scene with the general or whatever he was—she was dancing, right? Now how are you going to be a spy if you don't know how to dance?"

There must be some answer to this, thought Harriet as she sat there silently. She couldn't think of a thing. She went "Hmmmph" rather loudly. Then she thought of something. "Well, do I have to wear those silly dresses? Couldn't I wear my spy clothes? They're better to learn to dance in anyway. In school we wear our gym suits to learn to dance."

"Of course not. Can you see Mata Hari in a gym suit? First of all, if you wear your spy clothes everyone knows you're a spy, so what have you gained? No, you have to look like everyone else, then you'll get by and no one will suspect you."

"That's true," said Harriet miserably. She couldn't see Mata Hari in a gym suit either.

"Now"—Ole Golly stood up—"you better march downstairs and tell them you changed your mind."

"What'll I say?" Harriet felt embarrassed.

"Just say you've changed your mind."

Harriet stood up resolutely and marched down the steps to the dining room. Her parents were having coffee. She stood in the doorway and said in a loud voice, "I've changed my mind!" They looked at her

73

in a startled way. She turned and left the doorway abruptly. There was nothing further to be said. As she went back up the steps she heard them burst out laughing and then her father say, "Boy, that Miss Golly is magic, sheer magic. I wonder where we'd be without her?"

Harriet didn't know how to approach Janie about her defection, but she decided she must. At lunch Sport and Janie sat laughing over the new edition of *The Gregory News* which had just come out. *The Gregory News* was the school paper. There was a page reserved for every grade in the Middle School and every grade in the Upper School. The Lower School were such idiots they didn't need a page.

"Look at that. It's ridiculous." Janie was talking about Marion Hawthorne's editorial about candy wrappers everywhere.

"She just did that because Miss Whitehead talked about them on opening day," Harriet sneered.

"Well, what else? She hasn't got the sense to think of anything original." Sport bit into a hard-boiled egg. Sport made his own lunch and it was usually hard-boiled eggs.

"But it's so dumb and boring," Harriet said. "Listen to this: 'We must not drop our candy wrappers on the ground. They must be put into the wastebaskets provided for this purpose.' It's not even news; we hear it practically every day."

"I'll put *her* in a wastebasket," said Janie with satisfaction.

"My father says you have to catch the reader's attention right at first and then hold it," said Sport.

"Well, she just lost it," said Harriet.

"You oughta write it, Harriet, you're a writer," said Sport.

"I wouldn't do it now if they paid me. They can

have their dumb paper." Harriet finished her sand-wich with a frown.

"They should be blown up," said Janie.

They ate in silence for a moment.

"Janie . . ." Harriet hesitated so long that they both looked up at her. "I think they've got me," she said sadly.

"What? Was that sandwich poisoned?" Janie stood up. The egg fell right out of Sport's mouth.

"No," Harriet said quickly. Now it was anticli-mactic. "I mean dancing school," Harriet said grimly.

Janie sat down and looked away as though Harriet had been impolite.

"Dancing school?" Sport squeaked, picking the egg out of his lap.

"Yes," said Janie grimly.

"Oh, boy, am I glad. My father never even *heard* of that." Sport grinned around his egg.

"Well," said Harriet sadly, "it looks like I'm gonna have to if I'm gonna be a spy."

"Who ever heard of a dancing spy?" Janie was so furious she wouldn't even look at Harriet.

"Mati Hari," Harriet said quietly; then when Janie didn't turn around she added very loudly, "I can't *help* it, Janie."

Janie turned and looked at her. "I know," she said sadly, "I'm going too."

It was all right then, and Harriet ate her other tomato sandwich happily.

After school, when Harriet went home for her cake and milk, she remembered that it was Thursday and that Thursday was Ole Golly's night out. As she was running down the steps to the kitchen she was struck by a thought so interesting that it made her stop still on the steps. If Ole Golly had a boy friend and she went out on her night out—wouldn't she meet the boy friend? And . . . if she were to meet the boy friend—couldn't Harriet follow her and see what he looked like? Extraordinary thought. She decided that she would have to be extra careful and terribly crafty to find out when, where, and with whom Ole Golly was spending her free evening. If Ole Golly went to places like the Welsches did, like night clubs, Harriet wouldn't be able to follow. Out of the question. She would have to wait until she was Mata Hari for that.

But *IF,* for instance, this boy friend were to come to the house and pick up Ole Golly, *THEN* Harriet could at least see what he looked like. She decided to pursue this as she clattered down the rest of the way into the kitchen. Ole Golly was having her tea. The cook put out the cake and milk as Harriet slipped into place at the table.

"Well," said Ole Golly in a friendly manner.

"Well?" said Harriet. She was looking at Ole Golly in a new way. What was it like for Ole Golly to have a boy friend? Did she like him the way Harriet liked Sport?

"Well, iffen it don't rain, it'll be a long dry spell," Ole Golly said softly, then smiled into her tea.

Harriet looked at her curiously. That was one thing about Ole Golly, thought Harriet, she never, never said dull things like, 'How was school today?' or 'How did you do in arithmetic?' or 'Going out to play?' All of these were unanswerable questions, and she supposed that Ole Golly was the only grown-up that knew that.

"Where are you going tonight?" Harriet said abruptly. She couldn't think of any way to find out subtly without Ole Golly catching on. Sometimes the direct approach was best.

"Well," said Ole Golly, "that's actually none of your business, but I'll tell you this. I'm going out this afternoon at five o'clock, and by the time I get back, you'll be sound asleep."

I wouldn't count on that, thought Harriet. "Are my family going out too?" she asked.

"Yes, they are. You're stuck with me," said the cook in a grumpy way.

Harriet hated that. The cook never wanted to do anything in the evening except read the *Journal,* then fall asleep. Harriet hated the quietness of the house, the wholesale emptiness that seemed to envelop her as soon as the last door had shut, the last voice had called out gayly, "Go to sleep on time. Be a good girl." She didn't mind at all when they went out, if Ole Golly were there, because they always spent the evening playing checkers and watching television.

"How's the weather out?" asked Ole Golly unexpectedly.

"Right pretty," said the cook.

Hmmmm, thought Harriet. Maybe she's going to meet him someplace outside. Harriet got up from the table.

"Well," said Ole Golly, "guess I won't see you till tomorrow."

"Why?" asked Harriet.

"Well, you're going out now, aren't you?"

"No."

"No?" asked Ole Golly, considerable surprise showing in her voice.

"No," said Harriet, a tiny sense of triumph creeping into her voice. "I'm just going up to my room."

"Oh, well, I'll see you before I go then. I'm leaving about five," said Ole Golly and poured herself another cup of tea. Harriet left the room. Five o'clock. Perhaps she should station herself somewhere at five to get a good view of the front door. It was all *very interesting.* When she got to her room she wrote in her notebook:

77

WHERE DO PEOPLE GO AT FIVE O'CLOCK? SHE HAS AL-
READY HAD TEA. SO SHE WON'T GO OUT TO TEA. A MOV-
IE? OLE GOLLY DOESN'T LIKE THEM VERY MUCH. SAYS
THEY POISON YOUR MIND. THE CIRCUS IS IN TOWN. IF I
WERE MEETING SOMEBODY I WOULD MAKE THEM TAKE
ME TO THE CIRCUS. I LOVE THE FREAKS. IF I GO ACROSS
THE STREET AND HIDE BEHIND A TREE IN THE PARK I
CAN SEE THE FRONT DOOR JUST RIGHT.

At four forty-five she sneaked past Ole Golly's
room. She could hear Ole Golly getting dressed and
whistling to herself as she did. She must be in a good
mood to whistle, thought Harriet.

She found an appropriate tree and waited. She
waited and waited, looking at her watch every two
minutes. A policeman strolled by and stared at her.
She tried to look casual, as though she just happened
to lean against that tree all the time so what was he
looking at. Lots of taxis passed. She watched a woman
park her car. A delivery man on one of those bikes
with a cart in front parked in front of her house. She
looked to see if it were Little Joe Curry, but it was a
much older man with a little black mustache. He
went up to her front door. Suddenly it hit her. Could
this be the boy friend? She watched as he rang their
bell. He *must* be. Mrs. Welsch always ordered from
the Dei Santis and this man's jacket had another
store printed on it. The door opened and Ole Golly
came out. It *was. This* was the boy friend. Harriet
gave him the real once-over as he and Ole Golly stood
on the top step smiling and chatting to each other.

He was rather fat but in a round, hard, not un-
pleasant way. His head was completely round. His
teeth were very white under the trim mustache. His
skin was darkish, and the features of his face formed
a pleasant, round, cheerful image. He wore, naturally,
a delivery boy's coat, but underneath he wore nice-

looking gray flannel pants, and his brown shoes were shined within an inch of their lives.

He took Ole Golly's arm and they walked down the steps together, still smiling and talking and never taking their eyes off each other.

When they got down to the bottom of the steps the boy friend seemed to apologize for something, smiling awkwardly, then quick as a flash he took off his delivery jacket, reached into his cart, pulled out a gray flannel jacket, and put that on. He wore a bright blue tie and altogether Harriet thought he looked quite nice. He and Ole Golly smiled at each other, then started walking toward the park, leaving the delivery cart where it was in front of the house.

Harriet squatted down to hide herself more, and through a bush, watched their progress into the park. They were evidently going for a walk beside the river. They chose a path near Harriet, so she waited until they were a little ahead of her, then ran along beside them. She discovered that if they stayed on this path she could run along, completely hidden by the thick foliage, and, miraculously, hear every word they said.

"Mr. Waldenstein, have you ever noticed"—Ole Golly sounded terribly proper and enunciated everything quite clearly—"have you ever noticed how tidy the grass is in this park?"

"Yes, Miss Golly. This park is kept quite well. A lot better than that terrible Washington Square with all those creatures lying all over the grass. Make a pretty mess they do." Mr. Waldenstein had a pleasant speaking voice, although there was a certain amount of rasp and gravel running along the bottom of it.

"Yes. I always find it such a pleasure to walk along the river this way. I particularly like to watch the tugboats." Ole Golly didn't sound one bit like herself. Her voice seemed much higher, as though she were floating a bit off the ground.

"A walk in the park is always a pleasure for me when I am accompanied by an attractive young woman like yourself, Miss Golly." Mr. Waldenstein leaned a little toward Ole Golly as he said this.

Harriet watched in horror as Ole Golly blushed a deep red that started from deep inside her scarf and rushed like a spreading river to her hairline. Well, thought Harriet, how about that!

"Oh, Mr. Waldenstein," Ole Golly managed to breathe, then tried to change the subject by saying, "Will you look over there at that boat? That *is* a large one for the East River."

"No offense was meant, Miss Golly." Mr. Waldenstein looked worried. "I only want you to know how much I enjoy these Thursdays we have been spending together."

The crimson zoomed up Ole Golly's face again, making her look exactly like a hawk-nosed Indian.

Big Chief Golly, Harriet thought, what is happening to you?

And something was definitely happening. Ole Golly was *not* Ole Golly today. Instead of being strong, tough, and totally in control, she looked as though she might faint. Harriet pondered on this as she watched them turn onto the esplanade which runs along the river. There was no way to follow them now without being observed, so she decided to run back in the grass and see where they came out. She could keep them in view even if she couldn't hear them. Before going she scribbled in her notebook:

LIFE IS A GREAT MYSTERY. IS EVERYBODY A DIFFERENT PERSON WHEN THEY ARE WITH SOMEBODY ELSE? OLE GOLLY HAS NEVER BEEN THIS WAY. I WONDER IF PEOPLE ACT LIKE THIS WHEN THEY GET MARRIED. HOW COULD SHE GET MARRIED? WOULD MR. WALDENSTEIN COME TO LIVE WITH US THEN? THEY COULD PUT THEIR CHILD IN

MY ROOM IF THEY WANTED TO. I WOULDN'T MIND. I DON'T THINK. UNLESS IT WAS A VERY NOSY CHILD WHO TRIED TO READ MY NOTEBOOKS. THEN I WOULD SMASH IT.

Mr. Waldenstein and Ole Golly were so far away they were beginning to look small, so Harriet closed her notebook and ran up and down the hills and across the paths until she had them quite close again. They were turning off the walk by the river onto one of the smaller paths, the one beside the mayor's house. Harriet crept along beside them. Now she could hear them again.

"Would it be your pleasure to attend a movie this evening, Miss Golly?"

"Yes, indeed, I think that would be a fine idea," said Ole Golly.

Harriet's mouth dropped open. Ole Golly *never* went to the movies, and here she was smiling and looking like it was a treat. Well! Harriet grabbed for her notebook.

IF SHE FEELS THAT WAY SHE CAN JOLLY WELL TAKE ME TO THE MOVIES SOMETIME.

"Is there something interesting playing?" Ole Golly's voice was getting higher and higher, funnier and funnier.

"I think that there is a very nice picture playing over on Eighty-sixth Street, one that you will like. But if you do not like that one when we get there, then there are three other movie houses there and you can take your pick. I had thought that we could have a nice dinner at the Bauhaus there beforehand if you would like that. If not, there are lots of other restaurants." Mr. Waldenstein said everything in a very gentle way, looking constantly at Ole Golly to

81

see if she liked what he was saying.

"Oh, I think that would be just lovely. It sounds like a very pleasant evening."

WELL, THAT TEARS IT. I HAPPEN TO KNOW THAT OLE GOLLY JUST CAN'T STAND GERMAN FOOD. SHE SAID TO ME ONCE THAT IF SHE SAW ONE MORE WURST ON HER PLATE SHE WOULD THROW IT ACROSS THE ROOM. THAT WAS WHEN WE HAD THAT GERMAN COOK BEFORE WE GOT THIS ONE. WHEN OLE GOLLY GETS HOME TONIGHT I BET SHE WILL LAUGH WITH ME AND SAY WHAT A TERRIBLE EVENING SHE HAD WITH THIS SILLY LITTLE FAT MAN.

They had reached East End Avenue again, so Harriet couldn't hear them anymore. She stood behind the tree and watched them walk toward the house. Then a *really* funny thing happened. Mr. Waldenstein got on his bicycle. Harriet thought for a minute that he was going off for a while to deliver things, but then her hair stood on end as she watched Ole Golly, with great agility and even more aplomb, hop onto the delivery cart. She sat, very straight and very dignified, while Mr. Waldenstein, puffing a bit, got the bike going down the hill. Harriet watched open-mouthed as they disappeared around the corner into Eighty-sixth Street. She was so astonished that she sat right down on the ground and wrote:

WELL, I NEVER. I'VE SEEN EVERYTHING. I BET OLE GOLLY IS EMBARRASSED TO DEATH. SHE IS REALLY GOING TO LAUGH WHEN SHE GETS HOME TONIGHT.

Harriet went back to the house. She did a little bit of homework, read awhile, then started to play Town by herself. She sat with her father and mother for a while when they got in, then went upstairs and sat with her mother while she got dressed to go out to dinner. Everything bored Harriet. She felt tired and dull in the head as she sat watching her mother. She decided to ask her mother questions to entertain herself.

"How did you meet Daddy?"

"On the boat going to Europe," answered Mrs. Welsch, struggling with her hair.

"I KNOW that."

"Well, why did you ask then?"

"I mean *how* did you meet him. How *was* it?"

"What do you mean? You mean how exactly? I was coming out of the dining room and I bumped into him. It was a very stormy crossing and he threw up."

"You mean he threw up all over you?"

"Not exactly all over me, just splashed my feet a bit." Mrs. Welsch laughed. "It wasn't terribly pleasant. He turned beet-red, apologized profusely, then passed out. He looked perfectly horrified the next time he saw me."

"Do people always turn red when they meet who they're going to marry?"

"Well, no, dear, I doubt it. You see he'd thrown *up*, that's why."

"I know . . . but I mean . . ."

"Well, what?"

"I don't know," said Harriet glumly. She couldn't figure out what to ask. "I mean . . . what does it *feel* like?"

"To have someone throw up on your feet? Not nice I can tell you." Mrs. Welsch didn't seem to be listening very hard.

"NO," said Harriet in an exasperated way, "I mean, what does it feel like when you meet the person you're going to marry?"

"Well, dear, you don't *know* it—*then,* I mean. . . ."

"Well . . . well, when do you know it?"

Mrs. Welsch turned around slowly and looked at Harriet. Her eyes were warm and she had a curious little smile on her face. "Are you considering it?"

"What?"

"Marriage."

"ME?" Harriet jumped up. Really, she thought, adults are getting sillier every year. "I'm only eleven."

"I just wondered," said Mrs. Welsch in a bemused voice. "You seem so worried."

"I'm not *worried*." Harriet squirmed around. What am I? she wondered. Just curious. "I just wondered what it felt like," she said, sulking slightly.

"Well"—Mrs. Welsch stopped putting on make-up and looked at her reflection with distant eyes—"I imagine it's different for everyone. I felt . . . I felt your father was the best-looking man I'd ever seen. The fact that he threw up made me want to laugh inside instead of being absolutely furious, which is what I would have felt with anyone else. And the next night when he wasn't in the dining room, I wondered if he was feeling dreadful and I toyed with the idea of finding out." She went back to her make-up in a businesslike way. "I haven't the faintest idea what anyone else feels."

My mother, thought Harriet, doesn't think about other people much. "If Sport threw up on me, I'd bash his teeth in," Harriet said cheerfully.

"Oh, no, you wouldn't."

"Oh, yes, I would."

"Oh, no, you wouldn't," said Mrs. Welsch playfully and turned around and tickled Harriet's stomach. Harriet giggled and fell off the chair. Mrs. Welsch got up and went to the closet. As she was putting her dress over her head she said through the cloth, "We've got a long way to go before you start thinking about things like marriage"—her head appeared—"thank God," she said as she pulled the dress down.

"I may not even *get* married," said Harriet dreamily from the floor where she lay stretched out, arms and legs wide. "I may go to Europe and meet a lot of generals."

"What?" asked Mrs. Welsch absent-mindedly.

"Oh, nothing," said Harriet.

Mr. Welsch appeared in the doorway. "Good Lord, you're not half ready," he said in a very irritated way, twitching his cuffs.

Harriet looked at her father in his tuxedo. Was he handsome? She thought to herself that she had never seen him throw up, so she didn't know what he would look like doing that, but maybe everybody looked the same doing that. She had seen Janie throw up once when they went to see a movie about a gorilla and Janie ate four candy bars and three bags of popcorn. It was awful.

"Why don't you go and get the car out, darling? I'll be right there." Mrs. Welsch was flying around the room looking for things.

Mr. Welsch was in a terrible grump. "All right," he said peevishly. Then in a rather stiff, formal way he said, "Good night, Harriet. Go to bed on time. Be a good girl. Don't make any trouble for Miss Golly."

"She's not here." Harriet sat up.

"No, dear, the cook; it's Thursday. Now, go get the car."

"Oh, ALL RIGHT," said Mr. Welsch and stormed out the door.

"Well," said Harriet. She could already feel the empty house descending around her ears.

She dragged her feet around, making patterns in the rug until Mrs. Welsch was ready and going past her through the door, leaving a trail of perfume behind her. She followed her mother downstairs and at the front door suffered herself to be kissed.

"Now be a good girl—"

"I know, and don't make any trouble and go to bed and don't read under the covers," Harriet said nastily.

Mrs. Welsch laughed, kissed Harriet again, and pinched her cheek. "That's right, dear, and have a nice evening." And she sailed out the door.

That's a new one, thought Harriet. She got her book and clumped down the steps to the kitchen. The cook sat reading the *Journal*. "Oh boy," said Harriet and sat down at the table.

"Ready for your dinner?" murmured the cook.

"YES!" Harriet shouted as loud as she could. The silence upstairs was deafening.

Harriet tried to stay awake until Ole Golly came in, but she couldn't. So the next afternoon, after school, she went to Ole Golly's room even before she went to the kitchen. Harriet had to be dreadfully curious to break routine in this way. She cornered Ole Golly in as casual a way as possible, standing in the doorway to block Ole Golly's descent to her tea.

"Well, what's this? Have you had your cake so soon?" Ole Golly smiled at her.

"No. Not yet. Uh, did you have a good time?" Harriet tried to sound indifferent.

"What? Oh, yesterday you mean? Yes, a *lovely* time." Ole Golly smiled quite broadly.

"You DID?" Harriet was astonished.

"Well, of course, why not? I went to a fascinating movie and had a very good dinner beforehand. . . ." Ole Golly started down the steps.

"What did you *eat?*" asked Harriet, leaning over the banister.

"A new kind of wurst I'd never had before, quite good, and good potatoes. Yes, it was a lovely evening." And Ole Golly disappeared around the bend.

Harriet stood there a minute thinking. Then she

went slowly to her room. She felt the urgent need to make a few notes before she went downstairs.

THERE IS MORE TO THIS THING OF LOVE THAN MEETS THE EYE. I AM GOING TO HAVE TO THINK ABOUT THIS A GREAT DEAL BUT I DON'T THINK IT WILL GET ME ANY-WHERE. I THINK MAYBE THEY'RE ALL RIGHT WHEN THEY SAY THERE ARE SOME THINGS I WON'T KNOW ANYTHING ABOUT UNTIL I'M OLDER. BUT IF IT MAKES YOU LIKE TO EAT ALL KINDS OF WURST I'M NOT SURE I'M GOING TO LIKE THIS.

She slammed her notebook and went downstairs.

That night, while she and Ole Golly were watching a movie on television and playing checkers at the same time, Harriet, thinking of Harrison Withers, said to Ole Golly, "If people are alone all the time, I feel sorry for them."

" 'That inward eye which is the bliss of solitude,' " said Ole Golly calmly.

"What?"

"Wordsworth. 'I Wandered Lonely as a Cloud.' "

"Well, don't you?"

"What?"

"Feel sorry for them?"

" 'How sweet, how passing sweet, is solitude'!"

"What?"

"William Cowper. 'Retirement.' "

"Ole Golly," Harriet said loudly, "are you trying to say something?"

"Yes."

"Well, what, then?"

" 'Solitude, the safeguard of mediocrity, is to genius the stern friend'!"

"WHAT?" Harriet screamed with exasperation.

"Emerson. 'Conduct of Life.' "

"OLE GOLLY"—Harriet stood up. She was really furious—"do you or don't you feel sorry for people who are alone?"

"No," said Ole Golly, looking up quizzically at Harriet. "No, I don't."

"Oh," said Harriet and sat down. "I do."

" 'This above all: to thine own self be true, and it must follow, as the night the day, thou canst not then be false to any man.' "

Sometimes, Harriet thought, I wish she would just shut up.

CHAPTER 6

On the next Saturday night Mr. and Mrs. Welsch were going to a very big party. They had been talking about it for days, and when they were getting ready to go out they were all in a fluster. Mr. Welsch was put out because he had to wear white tie and tails and couldn't find anything—like studs and things. Mrs. Welsch's dress narrowly missed not getting back from the cleaners in time, and altogether almost everything went wrong. By the time they left they were in a state of high grumpiness and Harriet was glad to see them go. Ole Golly entertained herself usually on nights like this by making some new recipe, like Lobster Thermidor or *choucroute garnie,* anything that neither she nor Harriet had ever tasted before. This Saturday, however, Ole Golly seemed in a funny mood.

Harriet bounced into the kitchen, saying, "Well? What are we having?" and Ole Golly just looked at her as though she had never made a new dish in her life.

"Uh, I got some club steaks, asparagus, and we'll have a baked potato. You like asparagus, don't you?"

She said all this as though she weren't listening to herself.

This was really strange. Harriet felt nervous. Ole Golly knew perfectly well everything Harriet liked and didn't like. Besides, she happened to love asparagus. Harriet sat down at the table and looked closely at Ole Golly. She didn't even answer the question about asparagus, as she really didn't see any need to. Ole Golly was checking the potatoes which were baking in the oven.

"What are we going to do tonight?" Harriet asked tentatively.

"What?" asked Ole Golly.

"Ole Golly, what's the matter with you? I said, what are we going to do tonight?"

"Oh, I'm sorry, Harriet, I didn't hear. I was thinking of something else." Ole Golly, Harriet could tell, was deliberately making her face bright and cheery because she didn't want Harriet to ask her what the matter was. "I thought we might sit down here in the kitchen and play a game of checkers."

"In the kitchen? But we *always* watch television when we play checkers. You said that both things were boring by themselves but if we did them together at least your mind was occupied a little."

"Yes," said Ole Golly and took the asparagus out of the freezer.

"Well! What do you mean, then, 'sit down here and play checkers'? There isn't any *television* down here." Harriet felt as if she were talking to a child.

"Well, I just thought, for a change, you know, we'd sit down here." Ole Golly kept her back turned to Harriet.

The buzzer on the service entrance rang.

"My, I wonder who that could be?" Ole Golly said in a light, strange voice and rushed so hard to the door she almost knocked over a chair.

Harriet stared in amazement as Ole Golly threw the door open to reveal Mr. Waldenstein, all dressed up in a good suit with a bunch of roses in his hand.

"Why, Mr. Waldenstein," said Ole Golly. She knew, thought Harriet, all the time.

"Good evening, Miss Golly, so very nice of you to invite me to dine with you, and . . ."—he looked at Harriet who shot him an outraged look—"and with your charming ward." He was obviously planning to say more, but Harriet was sending so many nasty looks in his direction that he stammered a bit and stopped.

Ole Golly took his arm and led him to the table. "Harriet," she said in the same strained voice, "this is Mr. George Waldenstein. Mr. Waldenstein, this is Miss Harriet M. Welsch."

Well, thought Harriet, at least she remembered the M! Harriet stood up automatically and shook hands with Mr. Waldenstein, who beamed all over his shiny clean face. His mustache glistened in the light and his shirt front was so white it was almost blinding.

"Well," said Ole Golly, "do sit down."

Harriet and Mr. Waldenstein sat down. Then nobody knew what to do. Harriet looked at the ceiling. Mr. Waldenstein smiled at Ole Golly, and Ole Golly hopped around the kitchen nervously. "Well, Mr. Waldenstein . . ." Ole Golly began, but Mr. Waldenstein held up his hand in protest.

"George . . . please."

"Oh, yes," said Ole Golly, giggling in a way that Harriet had never heard before and instantly hated. "George, then, would you like a drink?"

"No. I never take anything. Thank you very much though, Catherine."

Ole Golly seemed pleased with this answer. Harriet stopped looking at the ceiling and looked at Ole Golly. I wonder, she thought, why that fat ole Mrs. Golly named her Catherine. I have never thought about her being named Catherine, or about her being a little girl and going to school and being called Catherine. I wonder what she looked like as a little girl. Even though Harriet tried her best she couldn't for the life of her imagine that big nose on a little girl.

Harriet discovered suddenly that Mr. Waldenstein had been staring at her steadily for some time. She decided to stare him down. He looked back at her with such a look of innocent pleasure that she was disconcerted. He looked as though he were thinking about her. Although she hated to admit it, there was a look of intelligence in his eyes. He leaned toward her.

"I think we have a friend in common, Harriet."

Uh-oh, though Harriet, he's trying to make friends.

"Who's that?" she said in a very unconcerned way.

"Little Joe Curry," Mr. Waldenstein said simply, then beamed in obvious pleasure at this feat of his.

"Really?" Harriet was very surprised.

"Yes, Little Joe and I are in the same business, you know, and he and I had a talk wherein we discovered that we knew the same charming little girl."

Oh, thought Harriet, if adults would only learn how obvious they are.

"He says that he has seen you many times on his delivery trips," continued Mr. Waldenstein.

"He certainly eats a lot."

"Does he? Yes, I imagine he would. He is a growing boy."

"Well . . . he hasn't seen me anyplace else, has he?"

"What do you mean, anyplace else?"

"Anyplace else, that's all."

"He sees you walking home from school."

"Oh." Harriet felt relief. She sat looking at the table top. Somehow she felt that now she was equally responsible for keeping this limping conversation on its feet and this irritated her.

"Little Joe Curry is a profound enigma to me, Catherine." Mr. Waldenstein leaned back expansively, obviously feeling that he had conquered the enemy and could now relax. "He has no other ambition than to be a delivery boy. After all, to me this makes very little sense."

"That's because you have known another life," said Ole Golly and smiled at him.

Harriet wondered what other life Mr. Waldenstein had known.

"Yes," he said, turning to Harriet, "it is one thing to come to this the way I have, to give myself time to think, and another thing to just be this all your life and never want more. I had a big business, you see, Harriet. Once long ago I had a very big business. I was a jeweler. I made a lot of money. I had a wife and a son, and my wife went to Florida every year with my son. I had a lot of money and I was the most miserable man alive." He looked at Harriet as though he expected absolution. She said nothing at all but looked straight at him. "I had a terrible ulcer, terrible pains every time I ate or drank. Life was worth nothing. It was so much dust in my hands. And then . . ." Mr. Waldenstein looked off into space as though he had forgotten what he was going to say.

"Life is very strange," said Ole Golly gently. This was one of her favorite expressions, and hearing it, Harriet felt somehow reassured.

"Yes," said Mr. Waldenstein and then, having recovered himself, he continued. "I saw that life was going to be dust if I kept it up, always dust, nothing more. And so I told my wife to take all the money and my son too. I told her that if she wanted to come with me and start over she could. But she didn't." A harshness crept into his voice. "She didn't. Well, that was her choice. We all make choices."

"Every minute of every day," Ole Golly intoned.

"And so I became a delivery boy. And suddenly life was sweet." Mr. Waldenstein let out a ringing little laugh, the laugh of a happy child.

"Well," said Harriet, because she could think of nothing else.

"It must have taken a lot of courage," said Ole Golly, bending over the stove.

"No," said Mr. Waldenstein, "—desperation."

Suddenly Harriet liked him. She couldn't think why, but she did.

"And now . . ." —he had a funny, shy smile on his face—"now I have some news. I have been thinking about two living as one. . . . I have some good news. I am promoted to cashier. I start next week."

"Why, that's wonderful!" Ole Golly turned with a big smile, and Harriet saw with surprise that there were tears glistening at the corner of her eyes. "Isn't that wonderful, Harriet? We must celebrate."

"I should think it would be more fun riding the bike than all those numbers," said Harriet.

Mr. Waldenstein threw back his head and laughed. "And I have thought as you, Harriet, all this time. I needed that time"—he considered a second—"but now, now I have had my time to think. I know that it will never be dust again. Never. And so I can work harder, and climb a little, and have a little more"— he held up his hand—"not *much* more, but a little, because I have—I have myself now. I know the value . . . the value of things." He tried desperately to express himself.

"Well," said Harriet again.

"Well, now," said Ole Golly. "How about some dinner now?" and she began putting dinner on the table.

Mr. Waldenstein watched her warmly, appreciatively. When she had finished and they were all eating, he said, "I would like to suggest a celebration. I would

95

like to suggest taking you two charming ladies to the cinema," and he smiled sweetly at both of them.

"Oh, no, we couldn't do that." Ole Golly looked very stern.

"Why not, why not? Come on, Ole Golly, let's go." Harriet wanted suddenly, desperately to go. She felt Mr. Waldenstein deserved something, and besides she never got to go to the movies.

"Oh, no," said Ole Golly, "out of the question."

"Oh, dear," said Mr. Waldenstein. "And why is that, Catherine?"

"Why, it's obvious! I have my work too, Mr. Wal— George, and I am here with my charge for the evening. I must stay here. It would never do."

"Oh, of course, what a pity." Mr. Waldenstein looked terribly sad.

"But Ole Golly, they won't be in till late. You know that. When Daddy wears a white tie they're never in until real late. You told me that." Harriet felt prepared to beg all night.

"After all, Catherine, no harm is done by it. Perhaps for once. . . ." He smiled so sweetly. "And it would give me such pleasure."

Ole Golly blushed again, deeply. Flustered suddenly, she got up quickly and went to the refrigerator. "I forgot your milk, Harriet. And would you like coffee or tea, George? I've forgotten to give us anything to drink."

"Can I have a coke instead?" asked Harriet.

"No," said Ole Golly. "You will have milk."

"But it's got radiation in it."

"So have you got it in you. You're having milk." This was the Ole Golly Harriet knew—stern, uncompromising. It made Harriet feel comfortable.

"If some danger were to come to the child, I would understand, Catherine, but as it is—a simple movie, a soda perhaps afterward at the drugstore—no harm will

96

come," Mr. Waldenstein pleaded simply.

"Oh, boy," said Harriet and jumped up from the table. "I'll go get the paper and see what's playing."

She ran upstairs to the library and went through the paper quickly to see what she wanted to see first before they got hold of it. She studied the paper thoroughly. She was torn between a spooky thing about children with funny eyes and a spectacular about the Greek gods. She decided that it was the better part of wisdom to suggest the latter. Anyway, it was in color. She ran to the kitchen, yelling the whole way.

"Look, look, Ole Golly, look, it's just perfect. It's what I'm studying and I like Apollo and Athena the best, look, I can learn all about them." When she hit the kitchen she noticed a change. Mr. Waldenstein and Ole Golly were looking into each other's eyes. They both had perfectly ridiculous expressions on their faces. They didn't even seem to have heard her. Ole Golly looked up dreamily.

"It's all decided, Harriet. We're going to the movies," she said sweetly.

"Oh, BOY," said Harriet and sat down and gobbled up the rest of her dinner.

"Not so fast"—Mr. Waldenstein laughed—"the movie will be there."

Harriet noticed that she was the only one eating. Evidently they both had no appetite that night. "See, here are the starting times," she said nervously, because she had the feeling that if she didn't get them out the door they would forget all about it.

Ole Golly looked at the paper. "I suppose we should go to the early show, just to be safe," she said.

"Goody," said Harriet, and finishing her dinner in a whirl, she jumped up and raced upstairs for her coat.

When she got downstairs again, they both had their coats on. The three of them went out the back door, around to the front of the house, and there they stood in confusion, confronted by the delivery bike.

Mr. Waldenstein didn't seem worried. "Ah," he said, "it's very simple. I have washed thoroughly the inside today, and Harriet will just fit. Catherine has already proven her adeptness at riding on the top."

"We could just take the bus," said Ole Golly nervously.

"Oh, no, let's do this, Ole Golly, please. I *want* to ride in it." Harriet jumped up and down on one foot.

Ole Golly finally relented and went back and got a blanket with which she lined the inside. Harriet found it very cosy when she got in. When the lid started to come down she said hurriedly, "Can I breathe?" Mr. Waldenstein then showed her the holes for ventilation and she felt better. The lid closed. Harriet heard Ole Golly jump on top. Then Mr. Waldenstein pushed off from the curb and they were off. They whirled down the hill and zoomed around into Eighty-sixth Street. It was terribly exciting. Harriet could hear all the traffic noises and Ole Golly and Mr. Waldenstein's conversation as they yelled to be heard over the noise.

"I'm the happiest man alive, Catherine," he yelled.

"Look out for that truck," yelled Ole Golly.

"Don't worry! I have precious bundles," shrieked Mr. Waldenstein.

"I think that's it ahead."

"Yes, I see," he screamed.

"Where can you park?"

"Oh, anywhere. That is the one advantage of this method of transportation." They were slowing down. Then they stopped. Harriet popped up like a jack-in-the-box as soon as she heard Ole Golly get off. They all laughed together because it was so much fun.

Harriet thought the movie was a gas. Zeus was very angry all the time and made a lot of temples fall over every time something displeased him. Paul Newman was Apollo and Shirley MacLaine was Athena. Harriet knew them from movie-star pictures her father brought home for her. She looked over every now and then to see how Ole Golly was liking it, but she didn't even seem to be watching much. They just kept looking at each other. It occurred to Harriet that maybe that was why Ole Golly didn't mind going to the movies. She never looked at them, so she might just as well be there as anyplace else.

Afterward they went to a drugstore across the street, and Mr. Waldenstein said she could have any kind of soda she wanted. She didn't really like sodas that much, so she had an egg cream, which she loved. They thought this was very funny for some reason, but she didn't care. They had giant sodas which they didn't finish, and they took so long that she had another egg cream. Then they went back to the bike and Harriet climbed in again. She felt so delicious that she almost fell asleep on the ride back. She could tell when they were almost there, because Mr. Waldenstein was having a terrible time pushing up the hill on East End. Then they stopped with a jerk and she knew they were home. Harriet heard Ole Golly say, "Oh, no," in an astonished voice, then she slipped off the cart. Harriet opened the top of the cart, and sticking her head up, saw with amazement that the front door to the house was wide open with light streaming down from the front hall onto the steps and sidewalk.

The three of them froze in their various positions, staring at the door. "Is it robbers?" said Mr. Waldenstein softly and started looking around for a policeman. He was still astride the bike, Ole Golly was still standing on the sidewalk, and Harriet was still poking her head out of the top of the cart, when suddenly there was a scream and Mrs. Welsch was standing in the front door, the light hitting the glittering stuff of her dress and making it sparkle.

"What IS this? What is the meaning of this? MISS GOLLY, I AM AMAZED!"

Ole Golly started toward the door, her arms open in the beginning of explanation. Simultaneously Harriet realized what must have happened. The Welsches had come home early. Oh, dear, she thought, we're in for it.

"Where is my child?" Mrs. Welsch was screaming hysterically. "Harriet, where is Harriet?" Ole Golly started to talk, still going toward her. "Is that you, Harriet? What are you doing in that thing?"

"Mrs. Welsch—" Ole Golly started but got nowhere because Mrs. Welsch turned abruptly back toward the house with a scream. "Come here, come here quickly," she called toward the open doorway. "They took Harriet someplace!"

"Mrs. Welsch—" Ole Golly was running now, horrified. She was on the top step by the time Mr. Welsch came to the door. The three of them stood framed in the light while Harriet and Mr. Waldenstein stared in open-mouthed astonishment.

"What in the world—" began Mr. Welsch, then ran down the steps two at a time and in one move lifted Harriet bodily out of the cart. "Who are you?" He breathed heavily into Mr. Waldenstein's face.

"I—I—we went—no harm meant, sir. Miss Golly and I . . ." Mr. Waldenstein looked terrified.

"Miss Golly . . ." Mr. Welsch said this in a terrible voice as he headed for the door with Harriet in his arms. Over his shoulder he said, "And don't you go away. Come inside here"—and he waited until Mr. Waldenstein had leaned the bike against the curb and was following him. He stood aside and let Mr. Waldenstein go ahead as though he thought he would run away. They went up to the doorway and Mrs. Welsch and Ole Golly moved inside ahead of them. Mr.

Welsch closed the door, and then all four of them just stood there.

Mr. Welsch put Harriet down, pushing her a little behind him as though to protect her, then said, "Now what is this business? Who is this man, Miss Golly?"

"He—this—" Ole Golly was speechless.

"I would like to take the trouble to introduce myself, please, sir," said Mr. Waldenstein, trying out his most winning smile.

"I wish you would. I don't like the look of this at all," Mr. Welsch said huffily.

"I think there has been some misunderstanding—" began Mr. Waldenstein.

"There isn't any misunderstanding. What are we all standing here talking like this for?" Mrs. Welsch was screaming at the top of her lungs. "Who is this man?"

She turned on her husband. "What are you chatting with him for?"

"Mrs. Welsch"—Ole Golly had her most dignified voice. "Mrs. Welsch, I would like to explain that no harm has come to Harriet. We simply went—" But she got no further.

"Harm? Harm!" Mrs. Welsch screamed. "What about the harm to me to come home in the middle of the night? Do you realize that it is twelve o'clock, Miss Golly? Do you REALIZE that?"

There was something about Mrs. Welsch's hysteria that made it impossible to combat. They were all floored by it as by a giant wave. She screamed on into the silence.

"I have NEVER had such a terrifying experience. I don't care *what* you did or *where* you went. This is *not* going to happen again. I tell you, Miss Golly, you are FIRED." The last word fell like a dropped tray.

There was utter silence afterward. Then Harriet burst into tears. Even as she did it she felt slightly ridiculous as though she were calling too much attention to herself. But she couldn't help it. The world was falling in pieces at her feet.

"*There!* There, you see the state of my child." Mrs. Welsch sounded melodramatic, even to Harriet, as she crossed the room and held Harriet's head against her side. "That is enough for me. You're fired and I want you to get out of here immediately."

Ole Golly said nothing. Her face registered total astonishment.

"Now, dear . . ." Mr. Welsch began, turning toward his wife.

Ole Golly drew herself up firmly. Her voice was level but Harriet could hear great feeling underneath. Harriet stopped crying to listen. "Mr. Welsch, Mrs. Welsch. I hope that you know me well enough by now to know that as long as this child is in my care not one thing could harm her in any way. If anyone were to try to harm her, they would have to do it over my dead body."

Harriet's eyebrows went up. This was impressive.

"I don't CARE. Don't you understand? You're FIRED." Mrs. Welsch stood her ground.

"Darling, let's talk about this reasonably," Mr. Welsch appealed to her.

"I am taking Harriet up to bed. She has seen enough for one night. If you want to discuss this further with this woman and this strange man you have never laid eyes on before, then go right ahead," and with that Mrs. Welsch marched Harriet right up the steps. Harriet tried once to twist away, but Mrs. Welsch had such an iron grip on her that she couldn't even turn. Mrs. Welsch marched her into her room, got her pajamas out, and started to take off Harriet's clothes.

"I can undress myself," Harriet said peevishly, "for heaven's sake," and she pulled her pajamas away from her mother.

Her mother was so distracted she didn't even seem

to notice this rude behavior. She didn't even say anything to Harriet but rushed from the room and down the steps again.

Everyone, thought Harriet, has gone nuts. What was going to happen to Ole Golly? Then she realized that she could hide on the steps and hear everything. She proceeded to do this immediately.

Leaning over the banister, she watched her mother go bounding down the steps. I have never seen her like this, thought Harriet. And she thought of a phrase she had heard her mother use about other people, "outlandish behavior." Was this outlandish behavior? From where Harriet sat, her head poked between the uprights of the banister, she could see Ole Golly, Mr. Waldenstein, and her father discussing the situation in whispered gestures, which stopped abruptly when Mrs. Welsch dove into the scene.

"I hope you've arrived at something!" Mrs. Welsch's voice had a most peculiar tremble to it. "I certainly hope you don't think you've done something behind my back, because I want you to know you're not going to get away with it." This was addressed to Mr. Welsch, who answered with a blank look.

"Mrs. Welsch—" Mr. Waldenstein was smiling in a terribly ingratiating manner.

"I don't even know who you *are,*" said Mrs. Welsch rudely.

"Darling"—Mr. Welsch went over to his wife and put his arm around her—"this is Mr. Waldenstein and he and Miss Golly have something to tell us."

Before Mrs. Welsch could get her mouth open, Mr. Waldenstein held up his hand to get attention. He then started, calmly and solidly, to speak in a way that held this attention. "Mrs. Welsch, I know how upsetting this kind of thing can be. I have a child myself. . . ." His voice spread over them like butter on a burn. "I simply want to say that, unexpectedly for

104

all concerned, this misunderstanding does not have to be a tragedy. If it weren't for the fact that just this evening I had asked for the hand of Miss Golly in marriage and she has most kindly accepted me, the loss of her very pleasant place here with you would certainly be just that, a tragedy. But, as it is, I do not think that she need have one minute's unpleasantness about this. She has said to me that she would be leaving next month anyway. I only hoped, and I know I speak for her too in this, that the parting could be more amicable than this." He stepped back one step and by so doing indicated that he had finished.

Mrs. Welsch looked at him blankly, her mouth slightly open. Harriet leaned so far out she almost fell to the next floor. Ole Golly looked at the floor. Mr. Welsch moved closer to his wife. "Darling, it seems they only went to the movies anyway. Harriet *is* safe, you know." He said this in a warm, soft way, and then they all stood looking at Mrs. Welsch.

"But, Miss Golly, you can't *leave*. What would we do without you?" Mrs. Welsch accomplished this extraordinary about-face without so much as a flicker of embarrassment.

Ole Golly looked up, and Harriet saw a flush of pride on her face. "I thank you for that, Mrs. Welsch." She stood looking at Mrs. Welsch for a second before she spoke again. "I think, however, that in many ways the time has come. Not only for me, but for Harriet as well."

On the stairs, Harriet felt profound shock. Coupled with this was a tiny thread of excitement which ran through her at the thought that Ole Golly *must* mean that she, Harriet, was able to take care of herself. Is that true? she asked herself. And she had no answer.

Ole Golly held the stage. The other three looked at her in wonder. She seized her moment and spoke: " ' "The time has come," the Walrus said—' "

" ' "To talk of many things—" ' " Harriet knew the words so well that without a second's thought she found herself standing at the top of the stairs saying them. All heads turned toward her.

Ole Golly continued: " ' "Of shoes—and ships— and sealing-wax—" ' "

" ' "Of cabbages—and kings—" ' " Harriet found herself laughing down at Ole Golly's smiling face as they went on, alternating the lines.

" ' "And why the sea is boiling hot—" ' " Ole Golly had the funniest look, halfway between laughter and tears.

Harriet shouted the last with glee: " ' "And whether pigs have wings" '!" She had always loved that line. It was her favorite.

Ole Golly didn't leave until the next afternoon. When Harriet got home from school, Ole Golly was finishing up her packing. Harriet ran pell-mell into the room.

"When did he ask you? I was there the whole time. When did he ask you to marry him?" Harriet had been waiting all day to ask this.

"Well, remember when we were having the sodas and you went over to look at the books on the rack?"

"Yes."

"Then. It was then that he asked me." Ole Golly smiled at her.

"Well . . . well, what did it feel like?"

"What do you mean?"

"I mean, what does it *feel* like to have somebody ask you?" Harriet was getting very impatient.

Ole Golly looked toward the window, folding something absently. "It feels . . . it feels—you jump all over inside . . . you . . . as though doors were opening all over the world. . . . It's bigger, somehow, the world."

"That doesn't make any sense," said Harriet sensibly. She sat down with a plop on the bed.

"Well, nonetheless, that's what you feel. Feeling never makes any sense anyway, Harriet; you should know that by now," Ole Golly said pleasantly.

"Maybe—" Harriet knew as she said it that it was a baby thing to say but she couldn't help it—"maybe there's a lot of things I don't know."

Ole Golly didn't even look at her, which was reassuring for some reason. "Nonsense. You know quite enough. Quite enough for yourself and a great deal more than some people."

Harriet lolled back on the bed and looked at the ceiling. "Will Mr. Waldenstein be working right around the corner?" she asked casually.

"No. We have decided to visit his mother and father in Montreal. Then if we like it there, we might make our home there."

"MON-TREE-AAALLLL?" screamed Harriet. "Where's that?"

"Harriet, don't take on so. It's unbecoming. Besides, you know perfectly well it's in Canada. I remember when you found it out."

"I know. But I won't see you then." Harriet sat up.

"You've no need to see me. You don't need a nurse now. When you're big and you sell your first book, I'll come into the bookstore and get a signed copy. How 'bout that?" Ole Golly gave her old smile.

"Wow! You mean you'll ask for my autograph?"

"I guess you could put it that way. Anyway, I'll look you up sometime when you're grown, just to see what you made of yourself, because I'll be curious. Now help me carry this stuff downstairs."

Harriet jumped up and picked up things. "Are you going to be happy with Mr. Waldenstein?"

"Yes. Very. Don't forget that little bag over there."

And Ole Golly went through the door.

"Is it fun being married?" Harriet continued as they went down the steps.

"How should I know? I've never been married. However, I doubt if it's *all* fun. Nothing ever is, you know."

"Well, are you going to have a lot of children?"

"And love them better than you? No, never. I'm probably going to work a little more until he gets a little more money, so I'll be a nurse to someone, but there's only one Harriet, remember that," and Ole Golly opened the front door.

"Well . . . Well," said Harriet helplessly.

"You better get to work, you've missed a whole afternoon with your notebook." Ole Golly was looking up and down the street for a cab. She seemed to be in a hurry.

Harriet threw herself up on Ole Golly's neck, and putting both arms around, hugged with all her might.

"Good-by, Harriet the Spy," whispered Ole Golly into Harriet's neck. Harriet felt tears start in her eyes. Ole Golly put her down sternly. "None of that. Tears won't bring me back. Remember that. Tears never bring anything back. Life is a struggle and a good spy gets in there and fights. Remember that. No nonsense." And with that she picked up her bags and was down the steps. A cab pulled up and Ole Golly was gone before Harriet could say a word. She thought, though, as she remembered Ole Golly leaning down toward the bags, that she had seen one tear fall.

That night as she got ready for bed alone, after having taken her bath alone, she wrote in her notebook:

I FEEL ALL THE SAME THINGS WHEN I DO THINGS ALONE AS WHEN OLE GOLLY WAS HERE. THE BATH FEELS HOT,

THE BED FEELS SOFT, BUT I FEEL THERE'S A FUNNY
LITTLE HOLE IN ME THAT WASN'T THERE BEFORE, LIKE
A SPLINTER IN YOUR FINGER, BUT THIS IS SOMEWHERE
ABOVE MY STOMACH.

She turned out the light and went immediately to
sleep, without even reading.

BOOK TWO

CHAPTER 7

The next afternoon Harriet didn't get home until five o'clock. She had purposely stayed away all day, first following her spy route, then playing Monopoly with Janie and Sport. The game had made her irritable because she hated to sit still for that long. Janie and Sport loved it. Janie had all sorts of systems worked out for winning, and Sport was so passionate about money that they were kept continually interested, but Harriet couldn't keep her mind on it.

When she got to the top of the steps she stood still a minute, quietly. The house was completely silent. Her mother was out and her father wasn't home from work yet. The kitchen was so far away she couldn't hear the cook. She stood very still, listening.

It hadn't been this way when Ole Golly lived there. That was one thing about Ole Golly, thought Harriet; even if she didn't say anything, you were aware of her. She made herself felt in the house. Harriet looked toward Ole Golly's room. It stood vacant, silent, its yellow door open. Harriet walked toward it. Standing on the threshold, she looked into the neat emptiness. It had been almost this neat when Ole Golly was in it, but there had been flowers. Ole Golly had always managed to have a sprig of something alive in the room. There had been the big flowered quilt too, that Harriet bounced in. Ole Golly took the quilt, Harriet thought to herself.

She turned and ran into her room. For a minute she thought she would cry. Then she went into her little bathroom and washed her face. She thought to herself that there was no good in crying. Ole Golly wasn't coming back. Crying wouldn't bring her back.

She sat down to read. How I love to read, she thought. The whole world gets bigger just the way Ole Golly said it was when Mr. Waldenstein proposed. She felt a twinge in her stomach. Phooey on Mr. Waldenstein, she thought; why did he take her away? Am I going to cry anyway?

The front door slammed with a bang and Harriet knew her father was home. He always came home with a bang the same way Harriet did. She rushed out now, banging the door to her room behind her, and thumped down the steps, jumping on each one as hard as she could, then running until she ran smack into her father.

"Hey, there!" He stood there laughing and tall, his horn-rimmed glasses fallen over to one side from the force of the impact. He grabbed her and swung her up into the air. "Hey, you're getting too much for your old man!" Harriet scrambled down, laughing, and he set her on her feet. "How much do you weigh now?"

"Seventy-five."

"Fat lady, you tell 'em, fat lady." He was putting down his briefcase and taking off his jacket. "Where's your mother?"

"Bridge," Harriet said in a disgusted way.

"Bridge. What a bore. How can she play that fink game so much? And those finks she plays with!" He muttered away to himself. Harriet loved to hear him

114

jabber on like this. She knew he wasn't talking to her, so it was fun to listen.

"Whatcha do today, Daddy?"

"Finked around with a lot of pictures."

"Got any movie-star pictures for me?"

"Harriet M. Welsch, I have no movie-star pictures for you today. If I have one good thing to thank the Lord for today, it is that I did not have to gaze upon the jowls of an aging movie star. Anyway, those finks have given me such a low budget I doubt that I'll ever see another movie star."

Today was Monday, Harriet suddenly remembered. Ole Golly had once said to her, "Don't mess with anybody on a Monday. It's a bad, bad day."

Mr. Welsch wandered into the library, newspaper in hand. "How about a little quiet now, Harriet?"

"Who's saying anything?" She was, after all, just standing there.

"I have the distinct feeling that I can hear you thinking. Now run along until Mommy comes back."

Uh-oh, thought Harriet, this is a very bad Monday indeed. He walked over to the bar and began to mix a martini. Harriet tiptoed away. She suddenly remembered that she had a little homework to do, so she went back up to her room. She thought that she had better do it before her favorite program came on at seven-thirty. Her favorite program was the early movie. She didn't like any of the kids' programs. She never seemed to understand the point of them. They seemed so dumb. Janie looked at all of them and laughed her head off, but they left Harriet cold. Janie also naturally watched all the science ones, taking notes the whole time. Sport watched the sports news and the cooking programs, taking down recipes that might make his father eat.

Harriet sat down at her desk and pulled out her school notebook. There was an assignment she had

115

to do for math. She hated math. She hated math with every bone in her body. She spent so much time hating it that she never had time to do it. She didn't understand it at all, not a word. She didn't even understand anyone who did understand it. She always looked at them suspiciously. Did they have some part of the brain that she didn't have? Was there a big hole missing in her head where all the math should be? She took out her own notebook and wrote:

EITHER WE EACH HAVE A BRAIN AND THEY ALL LOOK ALIKE OR WE EACH HAVE A SPECIAL BRAIN THAT LOOKS LIKE THE INSIDE OF EACH OF OUR HEADS. I WONDER IF THE INSIDE LOOKS LIKE THE OUTSIDE. I WONDER IF SOME BRAINS, FOR INSTANCE IN PEOPLE WHO HAVE LONGER NOSES, I WONDER IF THOSE PEOPLE HAVE A LONGER NOSE PART TO THE BRAIN. I HAVE A VERY SHORT NOSE. MAYBE THAT'S WHERE THE MATH SHOULD BE.

She slammed her notebook and tried to get back to the math. The numbers swam in front of her. She looked over at a large picture of Ole Golly, in which teeth figured prominently.

She looked up as her mother came to the door.

"How are you, darling? Are you working?"

"No, studying."

"What are you studying?"

"Math." Harriet made a terrible face.

Mrs. Welsch came into the room and leaned over Harriet's chair. "What fun, darling. That was always my favorite subject in school."

Well, there you are, thought Harriet. Ole Golly wouldn't have said that. Ole Golly always said, "Math is for them that only want to count everything. It's them that wants to know *what* they're counting that matter." And that was it all right. If only those little

116

marks meant something besides just funny little marks on a piece of paper.

"Why, here, baby—this is simple. Let me show you."

Harriet squirmed. They could show and show and show and show, but it would never make a bit of difference.

Mrs. Welsch pulled a chair over and sat down happily. She soon became absorbed in the problem before her and forgot Harriet altogether. Harriet watched her working. When she was sure her mother was absorbed, she took out her own notebook and began to write:

MY MOTHER HAS BROWN EYES AND BROWN HAIR. HER HANDS WIGGLE AROUND A LOT. SHE FROWNS WHEN SHE LOOKS AT THINGS CLOSE. MY DADDY HAS BROWN EYES TOO BUT HE HAS BLACK HAIR. I DIDN'T KNOW SHE LIKED MATH. IF I HAD EVER KNOWN SHE LIKED MATH I WOULD HAVE FELT VERY FUNNY. I JUST CAN'T STAND MATH.

Harriet's mother looked up with a smile. "There," she said triumphantly. "Do you understand that now?"

Harriet nodded. Better that way. Maybe she wouldn't go into it.

"Well, wash your hands, then, and come down to supper."

"Can I eat with you?"

"Yes, darling. We're having an early supper tonight. Harry's beat and I've just about had it."

"Had what?"

"Had it. Had it— It's an expression. It just means tired." She went down the steps.

Harriet wrote in her notebook:

HAD IT. THINK ABOUT THAT.

* * *

That night when she went to bed she read half the night because no one thought to take the flashlight away as Ole Golly had always done. They'd let me read all night, she thought finally; and when she put out the flashlight, closed the book, and put them on the night table, she felt sad and lost.

Harriet awoke the next morning with the feeling that she had been dreaming about Ole Golly all night. She picked up her notebook without even getting out of bed.

I WONDER IF WHEN YOU DREAM ABOUT SOMEBODY THEY DREAM ABOUT YOU.

She lay there a moment thinking about that. Then she suddenly remembered that today was the day for parts to be chosen for the Christmas pageant. She wanted to be on time because otherwise she would get a rotten part. Last year she had been late and had ended up being one of the sheep.

Even though she hurried she still went through the same routine she went through every morning. She loved routine so much that Ole Golly had always had to watch her to see that she didn't put on the same clothes as the day before. They always seemed to Harriet to fit better after she had worn them for a while.

As soon as she was dressed she bounced down the steps into the dining room, where her mother sent her back upstairs immediately to wash her face. How could she remember all these things, she wondered. Ole Golly always remembered everything. After breakfast she took a few cursory notes—comments on the weather, the cook, her father's choice of tie, etc.— then got her books and walked to school. She took a few more notes as she watched people pouring into the school. Everyone always sidled up to her and asked, "What are you writing in that notebook?" Harriet would just smile slyly. It drove them crazy.

Harriet always did her work swiftly and in a very routine way, signing everything Harriet M. Welsch with a big flourish. She loved to write her name. She loved to write anything for that matter. Today she was about to write her name at the top of the page when she remembered again that today was the day for discussion on the Christmas pageant.

Miss Elson came into the room and they all stood up and said, "Good morning, Miss Elson." Miss Elson bowed and said, "Good morning, children." Then they all sat down and punched each other.

Sport threw Harriet a note which said: *I hear there's a dance about pirates. Let's try and get that one, that is if we have to do it.*

Harriet wrote back a note which said: *We have to do it, they throw you out otherwise.*

Sport wrote back: *I have no Christmas spirit.*

Harriet wrote back: *We'll have to fake it.*

Miss Elson stood in the middle of the room and called for order. No one paid the slightest bit of attention, so she hit the blackboard with the eraser which sent up a cloud of smoke, making her sneeze and everyone else laugh. Then she grew very stern and stared a long time at a spot somewhere down the middle aisle. That always worked.

"Now, children," she began when there was silence, "today is the day to plan our Christmas pageant. First, let's have some ideas from the floor about what we would like to do. I don't think I need bother explaining what this day means to us. There is only one new child here who might wonder." The Boy with the Purple Socks looked horribly embarrassed. "And I think I can simplify this by saying that at the Christmas pageant we get a chance to show the parents what we have been learning. Now each one hold up your hand when you have a suggestion."

Sport's arm shot up. "What about pirates?"

"Well, that's a thought. I'll write that down, Simon, but I think I heard something about the fourth grade being pirates. Next?"

Marion Hawthorne stood up. Harriet and Sport looked at each other with pained expressions. Marion said, "I think, Miss Elson, that we should do a spectacular of the Trojan War. That would show everyone exactly what we have been learning." She sat down again.

Miss Elson smiled. "That's a lovely idea, Marion. I shall certainly write that down." Harriet, Sport, and Janie groaned loudly. Janie stood up. "Miss Elson. Don't you think there will be certain difficulties about building a Trojan horse, much less getting us all in there?"

"Well, I don't think we'll go that far in realism, Janie. This is still open for discussion anyway, so let's hear the other ideas before we discuss the details. I don't know how big a spectacular we could have in the time allotted us. Anyway, I think I should remind you that we are not supposed to give a play. The sixth grade is supposed to dance. We are due in the gymnasium in thirty minutes to discuss this dance with Miss Berry, the dance teacher, then be measured for costumes by Miss Dodge. Now you know that once the subject is chosen you all improvise your dances. But this year you will be allowed to choose your subject, whereas always before Miss Berry has chosen it."

"SOLDIERS," screamed Sport.

"Now, not out of turn, Simon. I'll go down the line and each one gets a chance." Miss Elson then called the role. "Andrews?" she said, and Carrie got up and said that she thought it would be nice to have a dance about Dr. Kildare and Ben Casey. Miss Elson wrote it down. There was a great deal of whispering around the room as people started trying to get their gang to agree on something.

"Gibbs?"

"I think that a dance about the Curies discovering radium would be nice. We could all be particles except me and Sport, and we could be Monsieur and Madame Curie."

"Hansen?"

Beth Ellen shot a terrified glance at Marion Hawthorne, who had been sending her a barrage of notes. Finally she said softly, "I think we should all be things you eat at Christmas dinner."

"Hawthorne?"

Marion stood up. "I think that's an excellent suggestion on Beth Ellen Hansen's part. I think we should be Christmas dinner too."

"Hennessey?"

Rachel stood up. "I agree with Marion and Beth Ellen. I think that's a good idea."

"Peters?"

Laura Peters was terribly shy, so shy that she smiled at everybody all the time, as though they were about to hit her. "I think that's a good idea too," she quavered, and sank gratefully back into her seat.

"Matthews?"

The Boy with the Purple Socks stood up and said in an offhand way, "Why not? I'd just as soon be a Christmas dinner as anything else."

"Rocque?"

Simon looked at Harriet. She knew what that look meant. She was becoming aware of the same thing. They were surrounded. They should have gotten together and now it was too late. In a minute they would all be assigned to things like giblet gravy. Simon stood up. "I don't know why we don't do the Trojan War like Marion Hawthorne said first. I would a whole lot rather be a soldier than some carrots and peas."

Very clever, thought Harriet. Maybe Marion would consent to her own idea. How bright Sport is, she thought.

"Welsch?"

"I think Sport's absolutely right" and sat down, intercepting a glare from Marion Hawthorne as she did so. Uh-oh, thought Harriet, she's on to us.

"Whitehead?"

Pinky's was the only name left. Sport threw a pencil right in his face. At first Harriet couldn't see why. Then she saw Pinky look at Sport, then stand up and say sadly, "I agree with Harriet and Simon."

Well, thought Harriet, that's three against the world. Too bad Janie had to be in such a hurry about the Curies.

There was a vote but they knew they had lost even before it happened.

Miss Elson said, "I think that's a lovely idea. Now we can have a little discussion with Miss Berry about which parts of the dinner we will take, and then you can start making up your dances at home. Now let's go to the gym."

Everyone but Marion Hawthorne and Rachel Hennessey looked terribly disgruntled. They all got up and filed after Miss Elson out of the classroom, down the stairs, into the courtyard, through the courtyard with the little patch of green called the back lawn, and into the gymnasium, where a scene of utter pandemonium greeted them.

It was obvious that everyone in the school was in the gym. There were all sizes and shapes of girls from little ones to older ones just about to graduate. Miss Berry was screeching frantically, and Miss Dodge was measuring so fast she looked as though she might fly right out the window. Hairpins were falling out and her glasses were askew as she whipped through waist after

122

waist, hip after hip. Miss Berry's leotards looked baggy.

Sport looked around wildly. "I've never been so terrified in my life. Look at all these girls." He began to edge his way toward Pinky Whitehead and The Boy with the Purple Socks.

Harriet grabbed him by the collar. "You stay right here. Suppose something happens and we have to have partners." She pushed her face close to his. He began to sweat nervously but stayed next to her after that.

"Now, children, sixth grade over here, please." Miss Elson was gesturing frantically.

Marion Hawthorne looked around pompously at everyone who didn't move instantly. She always seemed to be laboring under the impression that she was Miss Elson's understudy. "Come along there, Harriet," she said imperiously. Harriet had a sudden vision of Marion grown up, and decided she wouldn't look a bit different, just taller and more pinched.

"Boy, does she tee me off," said Sport, digging his hands in his pockets and his sneakers against the floor as though he would never move.

"Simon." Miss Elson spoke quite sharply, and Sport jumped a mile. "Simon, Harriet, Jane, come along now." They moved. "Now we'll stand here and wait our turn with Miss Berry and I don't want any talking. The din in this place is unbearable."

"Isn't it awful?" said Marion Hawthorne in a falsetto.

Harriet thought, Marion Hawthorne is going to grow up and play bridge a lot.

Pinky Whitehead looked as though he might faint. He ran to Miss Elson frantically and whispered something in her ear. She looked down at him. "Oh, Pinky, can't you wait?"

"No," said Pinky loudly.

"But it's so far!"

Pinky shook his head again, was dismissed by Miss

Elson, and ran out. Sport laughed. There weren't any bathrooms for boys in the gym.

"Thought he'd never leave," said Janie. She had gotten this from her mother.

Harriet looked at Beth Ellen staring into space. Harriet was under the impression that Beth Ellen had a mother in an insane asylum, because Mrs. Welsch had once said, "That poor child. Her mother is always at Biarritz."

"All right, children, Miss Berry is ready now." They marched over with flat feet like prisoners. Harriet felt like Sergeant York.

Miss Berry was in her usual state of hysteria. Her hair was pulled into a wispy ponytail, as though it were pulling her eyes back.

She looked at them wildly. "Sixth grade, yes, sixth grade, let's see. What have you decided? Well? What have you decided?"

Marion Hawthorne spoke for them, naturally. "We've decided to be a whole Christmas dinner," she said brightly.

"Lovely, lovely. Now let's see, vegetables first, vegetables . . ." Sport started to sprint for the door. Miss Elson pulled him back by the ear. Pinky Whitehead arrived back. Miss Berry turned to him, enchanted. "*You* will make a *wonderful* stalk of celery."

"What?" said Pinky stupidly.

"And *you*"—she pointed to Harriet—"are an ON-ION."

This was too much. "I refuse. I absolutely REFUSE to be an onion." She stood her ground. She could hear Sport whispering his support behind her. Her ears began to burn as they all turned and looked at her. It was the first time she had ever really refused to do anything.

"Oh, dear." Miss Berry looked as though she might run out the door.

"Harriet, that's ridiculous. An onion is a beautiful thing. Have you ever really looked at an onion?" Miss Elson was losing all touch with reality.

"I will NOT do it."

"Harriet, that's enough. We won't have any more of this impudence. You ARE an onion."

"I am not."

"Harriet, that is QUITE enough."

"I won't do it. I quit."

Sport was pulling at her sleeve. He whispered frantically, "You can't quit. This is a SCHOOL." But it was too late. A roar of laughter went up from the group. Even that mild thing, Beth Ellen, was laughing her head off. Harriet felt her face turning red.

Miss Berry seemed to come back to life. "Now, children. I think it would be nice to take each thing from its inception to the time it arrives on the table. We must have some more vegetables. You, there"—she pointed to Janie—"you're squash. And you"—she pointed to Beth Ellen—"are a pea." Beth Ellen looked as though tears were close. "You two"—she pointed to Marion Hawthorne and Rachel Hennessey—"can be the gravy. . . ." At this Harriet, Sport, and Janie broke into hysterical peals of laughter and had to be quieted by Miss Elson before Miss Berry could continue. "I don't see what's funny. We have to have gravy. You"—she pointed to Sport—"and you"—she pointed to Pinky Whitehead—"are the turkey." "Well, of all the . . ." began Sport and was shushed by Miss Elson.

After she had made The Boy with the Purple Socks into a bowl of cranberries, she turned to the class. "Now all the vegetables, listen to me," said Miss Berry, planting her feet firmly in the fifth position. Harriet made a mental note to make a note of the fact that Miss Berry always wore, even on the street, those flat, mouse-gray practice shoes. They were always terribly old ones with the cross bar curling away from the arch.

". . . I want you to feel—to the very best of your endeavor—I want you to feel that one morning you *woke up* as one of these vegetables, one of these *dear* vegetables, nestling in the earth, warm in the heat and power and magic of growth, or striving tall above the ground, pushing through, bit by bit in the miracle of birth, waiting for that glorious moment when you will be . . ."

"Eaten," Harriet whispered to Sport.

". . . once and for all, your essential and beautiful self, full-grown, radiant." Miss Berry's eyes were beginning to glaze. One arm was outstretched toward the skylight; half of her hair had fallen over one ear. She held the pose in silence.

Miss Elson coughed. It was a things-are-getting-altogether-out-of-hand cough.

Miss Berry jumped. She looked as though she had just come up out of a subway and didn't know east from west. She gave an embarrassed titter, then started afresh. "We'll start with the tenderest moment of these little vegetables, for you know, children, this dance has a story, a story, a lovely story." She trilled a bit of laughter to let them know she was still there. "It starts, as do all stories, with the moment of conception." She looked around in a delighted way. Miss Elson turned pale.

"It starts, naturally, with the farmer—"

"Hey, I want to be the farmer," Sport yelled.

"Do not say 'hey' to a teacher." Miss Elson was losing patience.

"Oh, but, dear boy, one of the older girls will be the farmer. A farmer must be taller, after all, than vegetables. Vegetables are very *short*." She looked annoyed that he didn't know this. Sport turned away in disgust.

"Well, the farmer comes in on this lovely morning when the ground is freshly broken, open and yielding, waiting to receive. When he enters, you will all be piled in a corner like seed waiting to be planted. You will just lie there in lumps like this—" and she fell abruptly to the ground. She lay there like a heap of old clothes.

"Come on, let's split; she's gone." Sport turned to go.

"Miss Berry, I think they've got the position," said Miss Elson loudly. Miss Berry turned one inquiring eye over her shoulder to face a royal snub from Miss Elson. She scrambled to her feet.

"All right, children"—she was suddenly crisp—"I want you to start improvising your dances, and I will see what you've done next dance class." The change in her was so remarkable that the children all stared in silence. "Please file over there and be fitted." She turned her back. It was all so swift that Miss Elson stood gaping a minute before she started to herd them toward the costume corner. They all looked back

curiously at Miss Berry, who stood, feet planted flatly, her misunderstood nose high in the air.

The costume corner looked like Macy's on sale day. Quantities of tulle flew through the air.

Sport wilted. "Boy, this is a scene I *really* can't make."

It *was* dreary. Harriet remembered it from last year as a long wait with your feet hurting while a terribly flustered Miss Dodge measured you in a sweaty way and, likely as not, stuck you full of pins.

"One day," said Janie, "I am going to come in here with a vial and blow this place sky-high."

The three of them stood glumly, staring at the tulle.

"How do you practice being an onion?" Harriet looked over at Miss Berry, who was falling into another pile of rags on the floor. Evidently all the dances were the same.

Sport got an evil look. "I think I'll scream as loud as I can when she measures me."

Janie's turn came. "Here goes nothing," she said loudly. Miss Dodge blinked her giant eyes behind her glasses, fluttered her tape measure, and dropped several pins from her mouth.

CHAPTER 8

When Harriet started her spy route the next day, she decided to visit the Robinsons first because the day before she had seen an immense crate delivered to their house and she couldn't wait to see what was in it. The Robinsons were always moody right before they bought something, and this time they had been moody for a week, so she figured this must have been a whopper of a purchase.

She sneaked up to the window. There was the crate. It sat squarely in the middle of the living room. How did they get it in? she thought, and then she saw that it would go through the door with just about an inch to spare all around. Mrs. Robinson was running around it in ecstasy. Mr. Robinson was hopping up and down on one foot. A Railway Express man was starting to unpack the crate.

"A crowning achievement," said Mr. Robinson.

"A joy, such a joy," said Mrs. Robinson, completing a circle.

"Wait till . . ."

"Just *think* what they'll . . ."

They were so excited they didn't bother to make

sentences. The Railway Express man ignored them. He worked steadily and noisily until the front section was ready to be pulled away. Harriet held her breath. The front panel came away, exposing nothing but sawdust. Well, thought Harriet, that does it. But then the sawdust was being pulled frantically away by Mr. and Mrs. Robinson who had leaped forward in their eagerness, pushing aside the Railway Express man.

"There! There!" screamed Mrs. Robinson. And there indeed was the strangest thing Harriet had ever seen. It was an enormous, but enormous—perhaps six feet high—wooden sculpture of a fat, petulant, rather unattractive baby. The baby wore a baby cap, huge white dress, and baby booties. The head was completely round and carved out of butcher's block so that it resembled a beautifully grained newel post with a face carved in it. The baby sat on its diapered bottom, feet straight out ahead, and fat arms curving into fatter hands which held, surprisingly, a tiny mother. Harriet stared.

Mrs. Robinson exclaimed with her hand to her heart, "She is a genius."

This was too much even for the Railway Express man, who could contain himself no longer and said, "Who?" rather rudely.

"Why, the sculptor. She is marvelous . . . she is brilliant . . . she is a white star in the firmament."

"Yeah? A dame made that?" He gaped.

"If you've finished . . ." Mr. Robinson looked pompous.

"Oh, yeah, yeah, I just have to carry out the junk. Where do you want her . . . it?"

"Darling, I still think the corner behind the entrance, so that it isn't seen *immediately*. You know, and then it will *dominate* the room from the couch."

"It'll do that, all right," said the Railway Express

man picking up excelsior in handfuls and stuffing it into the crate.

"Just be kind enough to remove this without comment," said Mr. Robinson huffily.

The baby was rolled into a corner and the crate removed by the grinning workman.

Harriet left Mr. and Mrs. Robinson holding hands and gazing at it in speechless joy.

She went to the street and wrote in her book:

OLE GOLLY IS RIGHT. THERE'S AS MANY WAYS TO LIVE AS PEOPLE, SHE SAYS. BUT WAIT'LL SHE HEARS ABOUT THIS THOUSAND-POUND BABY. OH, I FORGOT.

She paused and looked into space.

WHEN SOMEBODY GOES AWAY THERE'S THINGS YOU WANT TO TELL THEM. WHEN SOMEBODY DIES MAYBE THAT'S THE WORST THING. YOU WANT TO TELL THEM THINGS THAT HAPPEN AFTER. OLE GOLLY ISN'T DEAD.

She slammed the book shut, feeling something akin to rage. Then she got up and headed over to the Dei Santi family. Nothing much was happening in the front of the store, so she crept around to the back to watch Little Joe Curry.

He was in full command of an array of food that would have fed the Marines for a week. He munched happily. Harriet was wondering if the kids had been there yet, when suddenly the phone rang inside the store. Little Joe looked guilty and started to hide things, just in case, when there was a blood curdling scream from the front of the store. Little Joe was so startled a piece of bread fell right out of his mouth. Harriet dashed around to the front.

Mrs. Dei Santi was being held by Bruno in a half

131

faint through which she managed to scream as loud as a dying opera singer, *"Ecco, ecco,* he is killed—all is lost ... *Dio ... Dio."*

"No, Mama, just an accident . . ." Bruno began, looking helplessly to Papa Dei Santi, who was hanging up the phone.

"Dead, killed, truck smashed to bits, *eccolà ... Dio ... Dio ... mio figlio* . . ." And she swooned.

Bruno looked as though he might drop the considerable weight, so Papa Dei Santi rushed to help him. As he did so he said, "Mama, Mama, the truck is not smashed, Fabio is not smashed, nothing is smashed but his head when he gets here. . . . A fender, that's all it was—a fender."

Signora Dei Santi revived immediately and started to run up and down the store waving her arms wildly and screaming in Italian. The customers stood around like frozen food. She ran up and down, up and down, finally gathering so much momentum that she crashed on into the storeroom, there discovering Little Joe with a whole cucumber in his mouth.

"Ecco . . . not bad enough, stealing us blind . . ." and gathering up all the food in one arm and Little Joe by the ear, she came catapulting back into the store. The family stared open-mouthed. The customers came alive and started to edge toward the door, feeling that this was perhaps too much.

"Mama, Mama, *ti calma.* . . ." Papa Dei Santi, seeing the evidence of Little Joe's treachery, began to scream himself a long string of frightening-sounding words.

"But, Papa"—Bruno screamed to be heard—"where IS Fabio? Is he hurt? Is he in the hospital?"

"Him? Him? HE is fine. *Evidentemente.* What would happen to him? It's the TRUCK! The TRUCK is smashed." Papa Dei Santi managed to get this out, then went back to screaming at Little Joe. "Fired. You're fired. We not running a restaurant!"

Suddenly the front door tinkled, then slammed, and there was utter silence as they all turned to see Fabio standing there. He had a miniscule patch of plaster on his forehead.

"My SONNNNNN!" screamed Mama Dei Santi and rushed toward him. "You're HUURRRRRT! He's hurt, Papa, look, he's hurt." And she flung herself at him with such force that Fabio was hurled back against the door.

"It's nothing, nothing, Mama," he said, smiling. She straightened up, looked at him hard for one minute, then slapped him across the head. "Your FATHER work with his bare hands for that truck, work HARD, not like you, work HARD. Understand?"

The family watched this in awe as did Harriet. Fabio turned red and tears sprang to his eyes.

"Mama . . ." he began.

"Don't Mamma me. You no son of mine . . . no son of mine"—she raised one finger aloft to the ceiling—"from this—day—forward—"

"Mama," Papa Dei Santi interrupted, "don't. Don't yet. Let's see. Let's see what the boy has to say."

Harriet felt wildly curious.

Fabio shot a grateful glance at his father. He looked terribly embarrassed. He fidgeted in his pockets until he found an old bent cigarette, which he put in his mouth. It hung there broken.

Maybe, thought Harriet, he can't talk without that.

The whole family was looking at him. He bent his head apologetically, then began in a low voice: "I didn't want to tell you till later. I—Papa . . ."—he looked up at his father in a very sad way—"I just can't—I can't help it. I just don't want to be in the grocery business. It's not your fault. It's just . . . to be

133

stuck in a store all day . . . I don't—it's not for me . . . so I"—he took a deep breath—"I took another job."

"You WHAT?" Papa and Mama Dei Santi said in one breath.

"I took—I took another job. Only the only thing is . . . you need a car for this job . . . I'm a salesman." He looked frightened, Harriet thought.

"Well, well, well." Papa Dei Santi looked totally amazed. Then an enormous broad grin spread over his face.

"Son? You're—you're working?" Mama Dei Santi looked as though she might faint again.

"Yes, Mama." And looking at his father, he laughed. "I'm working."

"Santa Maria . . ." Mama Dei Santi fainted. Bruno caught her.

Papa Dei Santi uttered all sorts of exclamations and slapped Fabio rather hard, Harriet thought, on the back. The others gathered round, with the exception of Little Joe, who took this opportunity to filch a piece of gorgonzola.

Harriet tiptoed to the street and there sat down to write in her book:

MY, MY, BETTER THAN A MOVIE. IT'S SUCH A HAPPY ENDING I DON'T BELIEVE IT FOR ONE MINUTE. I BET THAT FABIO IS UP TO NO GOOD AS USUAL. WAIT, HE DIDN'T SAY WHAT HE WAS A SALESMAN FOR. I WONDER WHAT HE'S SELLING. I MUST COME BACK TOMORROW TO SEE WHAT HAPPENS TO LITTLE JOE CURRY.

Harriet went over to Harrison Withers'. She looked through the skylight. Harrison Withers sat at his work table, but he wasn't working. He was looking out the window. His face was the saddest face Harriet had

134

ever seen. She stared at him a long time but he didn't move a muscle.

She went across to the other skylight. There she saw such a strange sight that she almost keeled over. What she saw was an empty room. Not a cat in sight. She ran back to Harrison Withers to see if she had perhaps missed seeing the cats. No. Nor were they in the kitchen.

She sat back on her heels. They got him, she thought. They finally got him. She leaned over once more to look at his face. She looked a long time. Then she sat down and wrote in her book:

I WILL NEVER FORGET THAT FACE AS LONG AS I LIVE. DOES EVERYBODY LOOK THAT WAY WHEN THEY HAVE LOST SOMETHING? I DON'T MEAN LIKE LOSING A FLASH-LIGHT. I MEAN DO PEOPLE LOOK LIKE THAT WHEN THEY HAVE LOST?

CHAPTER 9

Harriet felt so grumpy she knocked off work for the day. That night after supper she tried to practice being an onion. She started by falling down several times, making a great bumping noise each time. The idea was to fall in a rolling way the way an onion would and then roll around in a complete circle several times, then roll slowly to a stop the way an onion would if you put it down on a table. Harriet rolled around and bumped into a chair, knocking it over.

Her mother came to the door. She looked down at Harriet lying there with the chair on top of her. "What are you doing?" she asked mildly.

"Being an onion."

Her mother picked the chair up off Harriet's chest. Harriet didn't move. She was tired.

"What in the world is all that noise I hear in here?"

"I told you. I'm being an onion."

"It's a pretty noisy onion."

"I can't help it. I can't do it right yet. Miss Berry says when I do it right, I won't make a sound."

"Oh, it's for the Christmas pageant . . . is that it?"

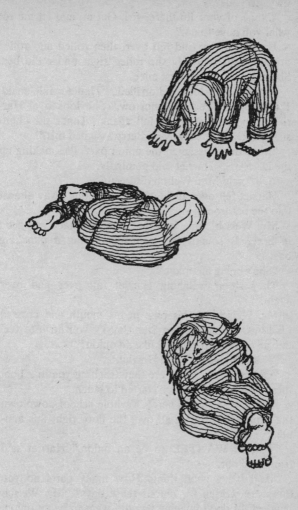

"Well, you don't think I'd just be an onion all on my own, do you?"

"None of your lip there, girl. Get up and let me see what you have to do."

Harriet got up and fell over, then rolled and rolled around until suddenly she rolled right under the bed. She came out full of dust mice.

Mrs. Welsch looked horrified. "That terrible maid. I'm going to fire her tomorrow." She looked at Harriet, who stood ready to fall again. "That's the clumsiest dance I ever saw. Miss Berry assigned this?"

"Miss Berry assigned the onion part. I'M making up the DANCE," Harriet said pointedly.

"Oh," said Mrs. Welsch discreetly.

Harriet fell over again, this time rolling away almost into the bathroom.

Mr. Welsch came into the room. "What's going on in here? It sounds like someone hitting a punching bag."

"She's being an onion."

They stood watching Harriet fall over and over again.

Mr. Welsch put his pipe in his mouth and crossed his arms. "According to Stanislavsky you have to feel like an onion. Do you feel like an onion?"

"Not in the least," said Harriet.

"Oh, come on. What are they teaching you in school these days?" Mrs. Welsch started to laugh.

"No, I'm serious. There's a whole school downtown that's probably rolling all over the floor right this minute."

"I never WANTED to be an onion," Harriet said from the floor.

"And it's a good thing. How many parts do you think are written for onions these days?" Mr. Welsch laughed. "I don't imagine you did want to be an onion.

138

For that matter, who knows if an onion does either."

Mrs. Welsch laughed up at him. "You're so smart. Let's see *you* fall like an onion."

"Don't mind if I do," said Mr. Welsch, and putting down his pipe, he fell solidly to the floor. The floor shook.

"Honey! Did you hurt yourself?"

Mr. Welsch just lay there flat. "No," he said quietly, "but it's not as easy as it looks." He lay there breathing. Harriet took another fall just to keep him company.

"Why don't you get up, honey?" Mrs. Welsch stood over him with a worried look on her face.

"I'm trying to feel like an onion. The closest I can get is a scallion."

Harriet tried to feel like an onion. She found herself screwing her eyes up tight, wrapping her arms around her body, then buckling her knees and rolling to the ground.

"My God, Harriet, are you sick?" Mrs. Welsch rushed over to her.

Harriet rolled round and round the room. It wasn't bad at all, this being an onion. She bumped into her father, who started to laugh. She couldn't keep her face screwed up and laughed at him.

Her father started being an onion in earnest, rolling and rolling. Harriet suddenly jumped up and started to write in her notebook:

I WONDER WHAT IT WOULD BE LIKE TO BE A TABLE OR A CHAIR OR A BATHTUB OR ANOTHER PERSON. I WONDER WHAT OLE GOLLY WOULD SAY TO THAT. OLE GOLLY LOOKED LIKE A BIRD WITH TEETH, BUT I THINK I REALLY LOOK A LITTLE LIKE AN ONION. I WISH SHE WOULD COME BACK.

Harriet was so absorbed in her writing that she had

forgotten her parents were in the room. When she finally slammed her book and looked up, they were staring at her in the strangest way.

"What were you doing, dear?" asked Mrs. Welsch in an ever so casual way.

"Writing in my notebook." Harriet began to feel nervous. They were looking at her in such a strange way.

"Oh. Can we see?"

"No!" Harriet almost screamed, then said more quietly, "Of course not, it's secrets."

"Oh," said her father and looked rather hurt.

What is the matter with them? Harriet thought. They both just kept looking at her.

"Is it something for school, dear?" asked Mrs. Welsch.

"No," said Harriet and felt even more nervous. Why didn't they stop looking at her?

"I'm sort of tired, honey. I think I'll go to bed," Mrs. Welsch said to her husband.

"Yeah. Me too," he said, taking up his pipe.

Why are they acting like that? thought Harriet. You'd think I was doing something very funny. Ole Golly never acted like that.

Her parents kissed her good night in a rather melancholy way and went out. She reached for her notebook and was starting to write when she heard her father say, *sotto voce,* on the steps, "Yes, it makes me feel I don't even know my own child." And Mrs. Welsch answered, "We must try to know her better now that Miss Golly is gone."

Harriet felt puzzled. She wrote:

WHY DON'T THEY SAY WHAT THEY FEEL? OLE GOLLY SAID "ALWAYS SAY EXACTLY WHAT YOU FEEL. PEOPLE ARE HURT MORE BY MISUNDERSTANDING THAN ANYTHING ELSE." AM I HURT? I DON'T FEEL HURT. I JUST FEEL FUNNY ALL OVER.

And by the time she went to sleep she felt even funnier.

The next day she felt very grumpy again on the way to school. Sport and Janie came running up to her as she was going in and told her that they planned to practice their dances that afternoon and did she want to practice with them at Janie's house. She said Yes in such a grumpy way, they stared at her. Then, when she breathed in a very labored way and said, "Don't mind me," they really stared. She went on into school, calling back over her shoulder, "I'll be there after my spy route." They just looked at her.

That afternoon she decided to try Mrs. Plumber again even though she knew it was terribly risky. She waited for the maid to leave the kitchen, then darted into the dumbwaiter, her heart pounding so hard she was sure it could be heard. She pulled the ropes gingerly. They worked smoothly at first, but just as she reached the parlor floor there was a terribly loud creak. She sat there horrified, not daring to breathe. Then she heard voices.

"Impossible . . . impossible." Mrs. Plumber's voice came out of a pile of pillows, in a whisper filled with horror.

"Nadine!" Mrs. Plumber screamed to the maid. "Nadine!"—a chilling scream fading at the end.

"Yes, ma'am." Harriet could see the maid standing primly to one side of the bed. Mrs. Plumber raised up, looking like a bloated eagle—"Nadine . . . it can't be, it can't beeeee"—and flopped back down, disappearing into pink pillows.

"Doctor's orders, ma'am."

From the pillows: "Confined . . . to . . . bed . . ." —and the tiny voice was lost for a minute—"for . . . the rest . . . of . . . my . . . life." And a wail arose.

Well, thought Harriet, feeling agitated and strangely

141

in sympathy with Mrs. Plumber. She did *want* to be there.

She moved a little to write in her book:

IS OLE GOLLY RIGHT? IS IT TERRIBLE TO GET WHAT YOU WANT? I WANT TO BE A WRITER AND I'LL BE FINKED IF I'LL BE UNHAPPY WHEN I AM. SOME PEOPLE JUST DON'T THINK THINGS OUT.

At that moment there was a querulous shout from Mrs. Plumber.

"What? What was *that?*"

Harriet looked through her peephole and saw both faces staring right at her. Her mouth opened in speechless terror. They had *seen* her!! She felt everything stop as in a photograph.

"There's nothing, ma'am."

But of course they couldn't have seen her. They couldn't see through walls.

"There's something in there! I heard it scratching, like a mouse—a rat . . ."

"Oh, I don't think so." Nadine marched firmly to the dumbwaiter and pulled up the door. She jumped and yelled wildly when she saw Harriet.

Harriet started pulling on the ropes. But Nadine recovered herself and stopped the dumbwaiter as it started to move.

"Come out of there, you," she said harshly and pulled Harriet out. Harriet flew through the air on Nadine's arm and landed in a pile at her feet.

"What is *that?"* Mrs. Plumber shrieked.

"A child, ma'am," said Nadine, holding Harriet by the hood of her sweatshirt.

"Out . . . out . . . get it *out* of here. . . . That's *all* I need—*all* I need today—a *child!"* And she fell back into the pillows.

143

Nadine hoisted Harriet into the air and swung her out the door and down the steps. Even though her feet were dangling helplessly and her mind was racing with fear, Harriet took a few mental notes of the interiors as they descended. "There," said Nadine, pushing her out the door, "good riddance. And don't get caught again in there."

Harriet looked back. Nadine winked at her. Feeling ridiculous, she started to run. She didn't stop running until she was at her front door. She sat down on the stoop and panted a long time. That's the first time in three years of spying that I've been caught, she thought. After she got her breath back she opened up her notebook.

SPIES—SHOULD NOT GET CAUGHT. THAT IS THE ONE ESSENTIAL THING ABOUT SPIES. I AM A ROTTEN SPY. OF COURSE, HOW WAS I TO KNOW SHE WAS GOING TO DO THAT? BUT THAT'S NO EXCUSE. I KNEW, I JUST KNEW IT WAS TOO DANGEROUS TO GO THERE.

She sat, looking dejectedly at the park. As she stared at the black trees one tear rolled down her cheek. She wrote:

OLE GOLLY WOULD HAVE HAD SOMETHING TO SAY ABOUT THIS. AND ALSO ABOUT THAT ONION BUSINESS LAST NIGHT.

She slammed her book, suddenly terribly grumpy. She decided to go over to Janie's house to practice, even though she had no desire now to roll around on the floor.

When she got there she saw that Pinky Whitehead and Carrie Andrews were there too. She went over to Janie and whispered in her ear, "What is HE doing here? Pinky Whitehead is all I need today."

"I can't help it," Janie said apologetically. "Carrie Andrews is the middle and Sport and Pinky are the two legs on the turkey. They all HAVE to be together to practice."

"Well"—and Harriet suddenly felt terribly evil— "I don't LIKE it."

Janie looked at her in the strangest way. "What do you mean you don't like it?"

"I just don't like it, that's all," Harriet said mysteriously and moved away. She saw Janie looking at her in a terribly irritated way a few minutes later, but that might have been because Harriet had almost rolled into the lab table. Janie was trying to be a squash by lying in a sort of pulpy way flat on the floor. Every now and then she jumped a little as though the squash were being boiled.

"That's terrible," said Harriet meanly.

"What was that you said?" asked Janie from her flattened position.

"You look like you're burping."

Sport and Pinky, who were doing handstands on either side of a humped-up Carrie Andrews, collapsed in laughter.

"I don't know what *you're* laughing at, Sport; you look ridiculous." Harriet was in an oh-so-vile mood all of a sudden.

Sport looked at her wide-eyed, then said, "What do you think you look like, rolling around like that?"

"I LOOK LIKE AN ONION," Harriet screamed and immediately thereafter felt totally frantic as though she would burst into loud baby sobs any minute. She got up and ran for the door. As she was going down the steps she heard Sport say, "What's the matter with her?"

And Janie replied, "Boy, what a pill she was today."

Harriet ran all the way home and all the way up to her room, where she flung herself on the bed and cried with all her might.

That night she had a terrible nightmare. Ole Golly was rolling around on the floor and cawing like a crow. She kept coming at Harriet, and Harriet would run. Ole Golly's eyes were red-rimmed and a shining blue. Her face had black feathers suddenly and a big yellow beak with teeth. Harriet screamed in her dream. She must have been screaming in her sleep because her mother came and held her until she went back to sleep.

In the morning before school she wrote in her note-book:

SOMETHING TERRIBLE IS GOING TO HAPPEN. I KNOW IT. EVERY TIME I HAVE A BAD DREAM I FEEL LIKE LEAVING TOWN. THEN I FEEL SOMETHING TERRIBLE IS GOING TO HAPPEN. AND THIS IS THE WORST DREAM I'VE EVER HAD IN MY WHOLE LIFE.

CHAPTER 10

That day, after school, everyone felt in a good mood because the weather was suddenly gay and soft like spring. They hung around outside, the whole class together, which was something they never did. Sport said suddenly, "Hey, why don't we go to the park and play tag?"

Harriet was late for her spying, but she thought she would just play one game and then leave. They all seemed to think this was a smashing idea, so everyone filed across the street.

The kind of tag they played wasn't very complicated; in fact Harriet thought it was rather silly. The object seemed to be to run around in circles and get very tired, then whoever was "it" tried to knock everyone else's books out of their arms. They played and played. Beth Ellen was eliminated at once, having no strength. Sport was the best. He managed to knock down everyone's books except Rachel Hennesscy's and Harriet's.

He ran round and round then, very fast. Suddenly he knocked a few of Harriet's things off her arms, then Rachel tried to tease him away, and Harriet start-

ed to run like crazy. Soon she was running and running as fast as she could in the direction of the mayor's
house. Rachel was right after her and Sport was close
behind.

They ran and ran along the river. Then they were on
the grass and Sport fell down. It wasn't any fun with
him not chasing, so Rachel and Harriet waited until
he got up. Then he was very quick and got them.

All of Rachel's books were on the ground, and some
of Harriet's. They began to pick them up to go back
and join the others.

Suddenly Harriet screeched in horror, "Where is my
notebook?" They all began looking around, but they
couldn't find it anywhere. Harriet suddenly remem-

bered that some things had been knocked down before they ran away from the others. She began to run back toward them. She ran and ran, yelling like a banshee the whole way.

When she got back to where they had started she saw the whole class—Beth Ellen, Pinky Whitehead, Carrie Andrews, Marion Hawthorne, Laura Peters, and The Boy with the Purple Socks—all sitting around a bench while Janie Gibbs read to them from the note-book.

Harriet descended upon them with a scream that was supposed to frighten Janie so much she would drop the book. But Janie didn't frighten easily. She just stopped reading and looked up calmly. The others looked up too. She looked at all their eyes and suddenly Harriet M. Welsch was afraid.

They just looked and looked, and their eyes were the meanest eyes she had ever seen. They formed a little knot and wouldn't let her near them. Rachel and Sport came up then. Marion Hawthorne said fiercely, "Rachel, come over here." Rachel walked over to her, and after Marion had whispered in her ear, got the same mean look.

Janie said, "Sport, come over here."

"Whadaya mean?" said Sport.

"I have something to tell you," Janie said in a very pointed way.

Sport walked over and Harriet's heart went into her sneakers. "FINKS!" Harriet felt rather hysterical. She didn't know what that word meant, but since her father said it all the time, she knew it was bad.

Janie passed the notebook to Sport and Rachel, never taking her eyes off Harriet as she did so. "Sport, you're on page thirty-four; Rachel, you're on fifteen," she said quietly.

Sport read his and burst into tears. "Read it aloud, Sport," said Janie harshly.

"I can't." Sport hid his face.

The book was passed back to Janie. Janie read the passage in a solemn voice.

SOMETIMES I CAN'T STAND SPORT. WITH HIS WORRYING ALL THE TIME AND FUSSING OVER HIS FATHER, SOMETIMES HE'S LIKE A LITTLE OLD WOMAN.

Sport turned his back on Harriet, but even from his back Harriet could see that he was crying.

"That's not *fair*," she screamed. "There're some nice things about Sport in there."

Everyone got very still. Janie spoke very quietly. "Harriet, go over there on that bench until we decide what we're going to do to you."

Harriet went over and sat down. She couldn't hear them. They began to discuss something rapidly with many gestures. Sport kept his back turned and Janie never took her eyes off Harriet, no matter who was talking.

Harriet thought suddenly, I don't have to sit here. And she got up and marched off in as dignified a way as possible under the circumstances. They were so busy they didn't even seem to notice her.

At home, eating her cake and milk, Harriet reviewed her position. It was terrible. She decided that she had never been in a worse position. She then decided she wasn't going to think about it anymore. She went to bed in the middle of the afternoon and didn't get up until the next morning.

Her mother thought she was sick and said to her father, "Maybe we ought to call the doctor."

"Finks, all of them," said her father. Then they went away and Harriet went to sleep.

In the park all the children sat around and read things aloud. These are some of the things they read:

NOTES ON WHAT CARRIE ANDREWS THINKS OF MARION HAWTHORNE
THINKS: IS MEAN
        IS ROTTEN IN MATH
        HAS FUNNY KNEES
        IS A PIG

Then:

IF MARION HAWTHORNE DOESN'T WATCH OUT SHE'S GOING TO GROW INTO A LADY HITLER.

Janie Gibbs smothered a laugh at that one but not at the next one:

151

WHO DOES JANIE GIBBS THINK SHE'S KIDDING? DOES
SHE REALLY THINK SHE COULD EVER BE A SCIENTIST?

Janie looked as though she had been struck. Sport
looked at her sympathetically. They looked at each
other, in fact, in a long, meaningful way.

Janie read on:

WHAT TO DO ABOUT PINKY WHITEHEAD
  1. TURN THE HOSE ON HIM.
  2. PINCH HIS EARS UNTIL HE SCREAMS.
  3. TEAR HIS PANTS OFF AND LAUGH AT HIM.

Pinky felt like running. He looked around nervously,
but Harriet was nowhere to be seen.

There was something about everyone.

MAYBE BETH ELLEN DOESN'T HAVE ANY PARENTS. I
ASKED HER HER MOTHER'S NAME AND SHE COULDN'T
REMEMBER. SHE SAID SHE HAD ONLY SEEN HER ONCE
AND SHE DIDN'T REMEMBER IT VERY WELL. SHE WEARS
STRANGE THINGS LIKE ORANGE SWEATERS AND A BIG
BLACK CAR COMES FOR HER ONCE A WEEK AND SHE
GOES SOMEPLACE ELSE.

Beth Ellen rolled her big eyes and said nothing. She
never said anything, so this wasn't unusual.

THE REASON SPORT DRESSES SO FUNNY IS THAT HIS
FATHER WON'T BUY HIM ANYTHING TO WEAR BECAUSE
HIS MOTHER HAS ALL THE MONEY.

Sport turned his back again.

TODAY A NEW BOY ARRIVED. HE IS SO DULL NO ONE CAN
REMEMBER HIS NAME SO I HAVE NAMED HIM THE BOY

The Boy with the Purple Socks looked down at his purple socks and smiled.

Everyone looked at the sock boy. Carrie spoke up. She had a rather grating voice. "What *IS* your name?" even though by now they all knew perfectly well.

"Peter," he said shyly.

"Why *do* you wear purple socks?" asked Janie.

Peter smiled shyly, looked at his socks, then said, "Once, at the circus, my mother lost me. She said, after that, if I had on purple socks, she could always find me."

"Hmmmmm," said Janie.

Gathering courage from this, Peter spoke again. "She *wanted* to make it a whole purple suit, but I rebelled."

"I don't blame you," said Janie.

Peter bobbed his head and grinned. They all grinned back at him because he had a tooth missing and looked rather funny, but also he wasn't a bad sort, so they all began to like him a little bit.

They read on:

MISS ELSON HAS A WART BEHIND HER ELBOW.

This was fairly boring so they skipped ahead.

I ONCE SAW MISS ELSON WHEN SHE DIDN'T SEE ME AND SHE WAS PICKING HER NOSE.

That was better, but still they wanted to read about themselves.

CARRIE ANDREWS' MOTHER HAS THE BIGGEST FRONT I EVER SAW.

153

There was a great deal of tension in the group after this last item. Then Sport gave a big horselaugh, and Pinky Whitehead's ears turned bright red. Janie smiled a fierce and frightening smile at Carrie Andrews, who looked as though she wanted to dive under the bench.

WHEN I GROW UP I'M GOING TO FIND OUT EVERYTHING ABOUT EVERYBODY AND PUT IT ALL IN A BOOK. THE BOOK IS GOING TO BE CALLED SECRETS BY HARRIET M. WELSCH. I WILL ALSO HAVE PHOTOGRAPHS IN IT AND MAYBE SOME MEDICAL CHARTS IF I CAN GET THEM.

Rachel stood up, "I have to go home. Is there anything about me?"
They flipped through until they found her name.

I DON'T KNOW EXACTLY IF I LIKE RACHEL OR WHETHER IT IS JUST THAT I LIKE GOING TO HER HOUSE BECAUSE HER MOTHER MAKES HOMEMADE CAKE. IF I HAD A CLUB I'M NOT SURE I WOULD HAVE RACHEL IN IT.

"Thank you," Rachel said politely and left for home.
Laura Peters left too after the last item:

IF LAURA PETERS DOESN'T STOP SMILING AT ME IN THAT WISHY-WASHY WAY I'M GOING TO GIVE HER A GOOD KICK.

The next morning when Harriet arrived at school no one spoke to her. They didn't even look at her. It was exactly as though no one at all had walked into the room. Harriet sat down and felt like a lump. She looked at everyone's desk, but there was no sign of the notebook. She looked at every face and on every face was a plan, and on each face was the same plan. They had organization. I'm going to get it, she thought grimly.
That was not the worst of it. The worst was that even though she knew she shouldn't, she had stopped

by the stationery store on the way to school and had bought another notebook. She had tried not to write in it, but she was such a creature of habit that even now she found herself taking it out of the pocket of her jumper, and furthermore, the next minute she was scratching in a whole series of things.

THEY ARE OUT TO GET ME. THE WHOLE ROOM IS FILLED WITH MEAN EYES. I WON'T GET THROUGH THE DAY. I MIGHT THROW UP MY TOMATO SANDWICH. EVEN SPORT AND JANIE. WHAT DID I SAY ABOUT JANIE? I DON'T REMEMBER. NEVER MIND. THEY MAY THINK I AM A WEAKLING BUT A SPY IS TRAINED FOR THIS KIND OF FIGHT. I AM READY FOR THEM.

She went on scratching until Miss Elson cleared her throat, signifying she had entered the room. Then everyone stood up as they always did, bowed, said, "Good morning, Miss Elson," and sat back down. It was the custom at this moment for everyone to punch each other. Harriet looked around for someone to do some poking with, but they all sat stony-faced as though they had never poked anyone in their whole lives.

It made Harriet feel better to try and quote like Ole Golly, so she wrote:

THE SINS OF THE FATHERS

That was all she knew from the Bible besides the shortest verse: "Jesus wept."

Class began and all was forgotten in the joy of writing Harriet M. Welsch at the top of the page.

Halfway through the class Harriet saw a tiny piece of paper float to the floor on her right. Ah-ha, she thought, the chickens; they are making up already. She reached down to get the note. A hand flew past

155

her nose and she realized that the note had been retrieved in a neat backhand by Janie who sat to the right of her.

Well, she thought, so it wasn't for me, that's all. She looked at Carrie, who had sent the note, and Carrie looked carefully away without even giggling.

Harriet wrote in her notebook:

CARRIE ANDREWS HAS AN UGLY PIMPLE RIGHT NEXT TO HER NOSE.

Feeling better, she attacked her homework with renewed zeal. She was getting hungry. Soon she would have her tomato sandwich. She looked up at Miss Elson who was looking at Marion Hawthorne who was scratching her knee. As Harriet looked back at her work she suddenly saw a glint of white sticking out of Janie's jumper pocket. It was the note! Perhaps she could just reach over ever so quietly and pull back very quickly. She *had* to see.

She watched her own arm moving very quietly over, inch by inch. Was Carrie Andrews watching? No. Another inch. Another. *There!!* She had it. Janie obviously hadn't felt a thing. Now to read! She looked at Miss Elson but she seemed to be in a dream. She unfolded the tiny piece of paper and read:

Harriet M. Welsch smells. Don't you think so?

Oh, no! Did she really smell? What of? Bad, obviously. Must be very bad. She held up her hand and got excused from class. She went into the bathroom and smelled herself all over, but she couldn't smell anything bad. Then she washed her hands and face. She was going to leave, then she went back and washed her feet just in case. Nothing smelled. What were they

156

talking about? Anyway, now, just to be sure, they would smell of soap.

When she got back to her desk, she noticed a little piece of paper next to where her foot would ordinarily be when she sat down. Ah, this will explain it, she thought. She made a swift move, as though falling, and retrieved the note without Miss Elson seeing. She unrolled it eagerly and read:

There is nothing that makes me sicker than watching Harriet M. Welsch eat a tomato sandwich.

Pinky Whitehead

The note must have misfired. Pinky sat to the right and it was addressed to Sport, who sat on her left.

What was sickening about a tomato sandwich? Harriet felt the taste in her mouth. Were they crazy? It was the best taste in the world. Her mouth watered at the memory of the mayonnaise. It was an experience, as Mrs. Welsch was always saying. How could it make anyone sick? Pinky Whitehead was what could make you sick. Those stick legs and the way his neck seemed to swivel up and down away from his body. She wrote in her notebook:

THERE IS NO REST FOR THE WEARY.

As she looked up she saw Marion Hawthorne turn swiftly in her direction. Then suddenly she was looking full at Marion Hawthorne's tongue out at her, and a terribly ugly face around the tongue, with eyes all screwed up and pulled down by two fingers so that the whole thing looked as though Marion Hawthorne were going to be carted away to the hospital. Harriet glanced quickly at Miss Elson. Miss Elson was dreaming out the window. Harriet wrote quickly:

HOW UNLIKE MARION HAWTHORNE. I DIDN'T THINK SHE
EVER DID ANYTHING BAD.

Then she heard the giggles. She looked up. Everyone had caught the look. Everyone was giggling and laughing with Marion, even Sport and Janie. Miss Elson turned around and every face went blank, everybody bent again over the desks. Harriet wrote quietly.

PERHAPS I CAN TALK TO MY MOTHER ABOUT CHANGING
SCHOOLS. I HAVE THE FEELING THIS MORNING THAT
EVERYONE IN THIS SCHOOL IS INSANE. I MIGHT POSSI-
BLY BRING A HAM SANDWICH TOMORROW BUT I HAVE TO
THINK ABOUT IT.

The lunch bell rang. Everyone jumped as though they had one body and pushed out the door. Harriet jumped too, but for some reason or other three people bumped into her as she did. It was so fast she didn't even see who it was, but the way they did it she was pushed so far back that she was the last one out the door. They all ran ahead, had gotten their lunchboxes, and were outside by the time she got to the cloakroom. It's true that she was detained because she had to make a note of the fact that Miss Elson went to the science room to talk to Miss Maynard, which had never happened before in the history of the school.

When she picked up her lunch the bag felt very light. She reached inside and there was only crumpled paper. They had taken her tomato sandwich. They had *taken* her tomato sandwich. Someone had *taken* it. She couldn't get over it. This was completely against the rules of the school. No one was supposed to steal your tomato sandwich. She had been coming to this school since she was four—let's see, that made seven years—and in all those seven years no one had ever taken her tomato sandwich. Not even during those six months when she had brought pickle sandwiches with mustard. No one had even asked for so much as a bite. Sometimes Beth Ellen passed around olives because no one else had olives and they were very chic, but that was the extent of the sharing. And now here it was noon and she had nothing to eat.

She was aghast. What could she do? It would be ridiculous to go around asking "Has anyone seen a tomato sandwich?" They were sure to laugh. She would go to Miss Elson. No, then she would be a ratter, a squealer, a stoolie. Well, she couldn't starve. She went to the telephone and asked to use it because she had forgotten her lunch. She called and the cook told her to come home, that she would make another tomato sandwich in the meantime.

Harriet left, went home, ate her tomato sandwich, and took to her bed for another day. She had to think. Her mother was playing bridge downtown. She pretended to be sick enough so the cook didn't yell at her and yet not sick enough for the cook to call her mother. She had to think.

As she lay there in the half gloom she looked out over the trees in the park. For a while she watched a bird, then an old man who walked like a drunk. Inside she felt herself thinking "Everybody hates me, everybody hates me."

At first she didn't listen to it and then she heard what she was feeling. She said it several times to hear it better. Then she reached nervously for her notebook and wrote in big, block letters, the way she used to write when she was little.

EVERYBODY HATES ME.

She leaned back and thought about it. It was time

for her cake and milk, so she got up and went down-stairs in her pajamas to have it. The cook started a fight with her, saying that if she were sick she couldn't have any cake and milk.

Harriet felt big hot tears come to her eyes and she started to scream.

The cook said calmly, "Either you go to school and you come home and have your cake and milk, or you are sick and you don't get cake and milk because that's no good for you when you're sick; but you don't lie around up there all day and then get cake and milk."

"That's the most unreasonable thing I ever heard of," Harriet screamed. She began to scream as loud as she could. Suddenly she heard herself saying over and over again, "I hate you, I hate you, I hate you." Even as she did it she knew she didn't really hate the cook; in fact, she rather liked her, but it seemed to her that at that moment she hated her.

The cook turned her back and Harriet heard her mutter, "Oh, you, you hate everybody."

This was too much. Harriet ran to her room. She did not hate everybody. She did not. Everybody hated her, that's all. She crashed into her room with a bang, ran to her bed, and smashed her face down into the pillow.

After she was tired of crying, she lay there and looked at the trees. She saw a bird and began to hate the bird. She saw the old drunk man and felt such hatred for him she almost fell off the bed. Then she thought of them all and she hated them each and every one in turn: Carrie Andrews, Marion Hawthorne, Rachel Hennessey, Beth Ellen Hansen, Laura Peters, Pinky Whitehead, the new one with the purple socks, and even Sport and Janie, especially Sport and Janie.

She just hated them. I *hate* them, she thought. She picked up her notebook:

WHEN I AM BIG I WILL BE A SPY. I WILL GO TO ONE
COUNTRY AND I WILL FIND OUT ITS SECRETS AND THEN
I WILL GO TO ANOTHER COUNTRY AND TELL THEM AND
THEN FIND OUT THEIR SECRETS AND I WILL GO BACK TO
THE FIRST ONE AND RAT ON THE SECOND AND I WILL GO
TO THE SECOND AND RAT ON THE FIRST. I WILL BE THE
BEST SPY THERE EVER WAS AND I WILL KNOW EVERY-
THING. EVERYTHING.

As she began to fall asleep she thought, And then
they'll all be petrified of me.

Harriet was sick for three days. That is, she lay in
bed for three days. Then her mother took her to see
the kindly old family doctor. He used to be a kindly
old family doctor who made house calls, but now he
wouldn't anymore. One day he had stamped his foot
at Harriet's mother and said, "I like my office and
I'm going to stay in it. I pay so much rent on this office
that if I leave it for five minutes my child misses a
year of school. I'm never coming out again." And
from that moment on he didn't. Harriet rather respected
him for it, but his stethoscope was cold.

When he had looked Harriet all over, he said to her
mother, "There isn't a blessed thing wrong with her."

Harriet's mother gave her a dirty look, then sent her
out into the outer office. As Harriet closed the door
behind her she heard the doctor saying, "I think I
know what's the matter with her. Carrie told us some
long story about a notebook."

Harriet stopped dead in her tracks. "That's right,"
she said out loud to herself, "his name is Dr. Andrews,
so he's Carrie Andrews' father."

She got out her notebook and wrote it down. Then
she wrote:

I WONDER WHY HE DOESN'T CURE THAT PIMPLE ON
CARRIE'S NOSE?

"Come on, young lady, we're going home." Harriet's mother took her by the hand. She looked as though she might take Harriet home and kill her. As it turned out, she didn't. When they got home, she said briskly, "All right, Harriet the Spy, come into the library and talk to me."

Harriet followed her, dragging her feet. She wished she were Beth Ellen who had never met her mother.

"Now, Harriet, I hear you're keeping dossiers on everyone in school."

"What's that?" Harriet had been prepared to deny everything but this was a new one.

"You keep a notebook?"

"A notebook?"

"Well, don't you?"

"Why?"

"Answer me, Harriet." It was serious.

"Yes."

"What did you put in it?"

"Everything."

"Well, what kind of thing?"

"Just . . . things."

"Harriet Welsch, answer me. What do you write about your classmates?"

"Oh, just . . . well, things I think. . . . Some nice things . . . and—and mean things."

"And your friends saw it?"

"Yes, but they shouldn't have looked. It's private. It even says PRIVATE all over the front of it."

"Nevertheless, they did. Right?"

"Yes."

"And then what happened?"

"Nothing."

"Nothing?" Harriet's mother looked very skeptical.

"Well . . . my tomato sandwich disappeared."

"Don't you think that maybe all those mean things made them angry?"

162

Harriet considered this as though it had never entered her mind. "Well, maybe, but they shouldn't have looked. It's private property."

"That, Harriet, is beside the point. They *did*. Now why do you think they got angry?"

"I don't know."

"Well . . ." Mrs. Welsch seemed to be debating whether to say what she finally did. "How did you feel when you got some of those notes?"

There was a silence. Harriet looked at her feet.

"Harriet?" Her mother was waiting for an answer.

"I think I feel sick again. I think I'll go to bed."

"Now, darling, you're not sick. Just think about it a moment. How did you feel?"

Harriet burst into tears. She ran to her mother and cried very hard. "I felt awful. I felt awful," was all she could say. Her mother hugged her and kissed her a lot. The more she hugged her the better Harriet felt. She was still being hugged when her father came home. He hugged her too, even though he didn't know what it was all about. After that they all had dinner and Harriet went up to bed.

Before going to sleep she wrote in her notebook:

THAT WAS ALL VERY NICE BUT IT HAS NOTHING TO DO WITH MY NOTEBOOK. ONLY OLE GOLLY UNDERSTANDS ABOUT MY NOTEBOOK. I WILL ALWAYS HAVE A NOTEBOOK. I THINK I WILL WRITE DOWN EVERYTHING, EVERY SINGLE SOLITARY THING THAT HAPPENS TO ME.

She went peacefully to sleep. The next morning the first thing she did when she woke up was to reach for her notebook and scribble furiously:

WHEN I WAKE UP IN THE MORNING I WISH I WERE DEAD.

Having disposed of that, she got up, put on the same

clothes she had had on the day before. Before she went downstairs she began to think about the fact that her room was in the attic. She wrote:

THEY PUT ME UP HERE IN THIS ROOM BECAUSE THEY THINK I'M A WITCH.

Even as she did it she knew perfectly well that her parents thought nothing of the kind. She slammed her notebook and ran down the three flights of stairs as though she had been shot out of a cannon. She hurtled into the kitchen, collided with the cook, and knocked a glass of water from her hand.

"Look what you've done, you maniac. What are you doing running like that? If you were my child, I'd slap you right across the face. In fact, you just watch it, I might anyway," the cook spluttered in exasperation.

But Harriet was up the stairs again, out of reach. She had only descended to wrest a piece of toast from the cook instead of having to wait in the dining room. She stomped to her place and sat down with a thump. Her mother looked her over.

"Harriet, you haven't washed, and furthermore it seems to me those clothes look awfully familiar. Go up and change." Her mother said all this cheerfully.

Harriet was off and running again. *Clackety clack*, her feet went on the parquet floor, then *thrump, thrump, thrump* up the carpeted stairs. She ran all the way into her little bathroom. She had a fleeting sensation of being tired as she stood over the basin washing her hands.

The sun was pouring through the tiny window which overlooked the park and the river. Harriet stared, lost in a sudden dream. She turned the soap over and over in her hands and felt the warm water on her fingers as she watched a tugboat, yellow with a red stack, bob neatly up the river, the frothy V behind it curling into emptiness.

A bell tinkled somewhere downstairs, and her mother called up the steps, "Harriet, you'll be late for school." Harriet suddenly woke up and saw that the soap had become a big mush in her hands. She washed it all off then flew down the steps, drying her hands briskly on her dress as she went.

Her father was at the table behind a newspaper. Her mother was behind another newspaper.

The cook waddled in, muttering, "Scared the life out of me this morning. She'll kill us all someday." No one paid any attention to her. She gave Harriet a very nasty eye as she served her bacon, eggs, toast, and milk.

Harriet gobbled up everything very fast, slid off the chair, and was out into the hall without either her father or her mother lowering a newspaper. She grabbed up her books and her notebook. As she was flying through the door she heard the rustle of a newspaper and her mother's voice. "Harriet? Did you go to the bathroom?" All that came back to her mother was a long, distant "Noooooooo," like the howl of a tiny wind, as Harriet flew through the front door and down the front steps.

Once out of the house she slowed to a dawdle and began looking around her. Why do I run so? she thought. I have only two and a half blocks to walk. She was always early. She crossed East End at the corner of Eighty-sixth and walked through the park, climbing the small hill up through the early morning onto the esplanade, and finally sat, *plunk* on a bench right by the river's edge. The sunlight coming off the river made her squint her eyes. She opened her notebook and wrote:

165

SOMETIMES THAT HOUSE GETS ME. I MUST MAKE A LIST
OF WAYS TO MAKE MYSELF BETTER.

NUMBER (1) STOP RUNNING INTO THE COOK.

NUMBER (2) PUT DOWN EVERY SINGLE THING IN THIS
NOTEBOOK.

NUMBER (3) NEVER, NEVER, NEVER LET ANYONE SEE
IT.

NUMBER (4) FIND OUT HOW I CAN REALLY GET MY-
SELF UP EARLIER IN THE MORNING SO I
CAN GET MORE SPYING DONE IN THIS
TIME BEFORE SCHOOL. I AM SO DUMB AND
THERE IS SO MUCH TO FIND OUT THAT I
HAD BETTER BEGIN USING ALL MY FREE
TIME SPYING.

Just at that moment Harriet felt someone give her
a hard little clip on the shoulder. She looked up quickly
and there was Rachel Hennessey. She stood there
squinting at Harriet through her glasses. Harriet squint-
ed back at her.

"Writing again in that notebook, eh?" Rachel shot
this out of her mouth like a gangster. She stood squarely on her two feet, squinting.

"So what?" Harriet's voice shook. Then she got
control of herself. "So what if I am? Whadaya wanta
make of it?"

Rachel turned mysterious. "You'll see. You'll see
what you get, Miss Harriet the Spy." She pivoted slowly on one foot all the way around, then stood squarely
again, squinting. A prism of light caught her glasses,
so Harriet couldn't see her eyes.

Harriet felt it necessary to become menacing. She
slid slowly off the bench and in two steps was almost
nose to nose with Rachel. "Listen here, Rachel Hennessey, just what do you mean by that?"

Rachel began to get nervous. Harriet pressed her

166

advantage. "You know, Rachel, that you're KNOWN for never meaning anything you say. You know that, don't you?"

Rachel looked completely taken aback. She stood her ground, but she remained silent. Only her eyes, which watered suddenly, let Harriet know that she was afraid.

"All of you—all of you better stop acting this way to me or . . . or . . . you're going to GET it!" Harriet realized, too late, that she was getting carried away because her arms were flailing around.

Something stirred deep in Rachel. Perhaps this last remark had made her see that Harriet, for all her yelling, was frightened. At any rate, suddenly she laughed in a rather spooky way, and as she did she backed away. She continued to laugh and to back, and only when it was obvious that she was poised for instant flight did she say, "Oh, no, you don't. You're wrong there. We have a plan. It's YOU who's going to get it. We have a PLAN . . . a PLAN. . . ." and it echoed behind her as she ran, her heels flying up and almost touching the sash of her plaid dress, she ran so hard.

Harriet stood there looking into the silence. She picked up her notebook. She put it down again and looked out over the water. The sun had dimmed. It might rain. She picked up the notebook again.

A PLAN. THIS IS SERIOUS. THEY MEAN BUSINESS. IT MEANS THEY HAVE BEEN TALKING AMONG THEMSELVES. ARE THEY GOING TO KILL ME? IS THIS MY LAST VIEW OF CARL SCHURZ PARK? WILL THERE BE NOTHING LEFT HERE TOMORROW ON THIS BENCH? WILL ANYONE REMEMBER HARRIET M. WELSCH?

She rose stiffly and walked slowly to school. Everything looked very green and holy in that sad light before a rain. Even the Good Humor man on the corner, the one with the ridiculous nose, looked sad and moody. He took out a large blue handkerchief and blew his nose. It was somehow so touching that Harriet had to look away.

The door to the school was alive with clamoring children. She wished that she could wait until everyone was in, then walk sedately, alone, down the corridors as though to her own execution. But if she did, she would be late. She ran toward the school.

CHAPTER 11

That afternoon the rain beat like a spring rain against the windows of the math class as Harriet wrote:

THERE IS SOMETHING GOING ON. SPORT HAS A TOOL KIT HE HAS BEEN CARRYING AROUND ALL DAY. CARRIE ANDREWS' POCKET IN HER SWEATER IS FILLED WITH NAILS. EITHER THEY ARE GOING TO BUILD SOMETHING OR THEY ARE GOING TO CATCH ME AND DRIVE NAILS THROUGH MY HEAD.

She looked around at everyone, then went on:

EVERYBODY WHISPERS TOGETHER ALL THE TIME AND NOBODY HAS SAID A WORD TO ME. AT LUNCH I HAD TO EAT MY TOMATO SANDWICH ALL ALONE BECAUSE EVERY TIME I SAT DOWN NEXT TO THEM EVERYBODY GOT UP AND MOVED. I GOT TIRED OF MOVING SO I JUST SAT AND ATE IT ANYWAY.

She looked around again.

THERE IS SOMETHING THE MATTER WITH THESE PEOPLE.

RACHEL HENNESSEY STARES AT ME ALL THE TIME WITH A TERRIBLE LOOK ON HER FACE. WHEN I WAS IN THE BATHROOM THEY DIDN'T KNOW I WAS IN THERE AND I HEARD CARRIE TELL RACHEL THAT SHE COULDN'T BE AT RACHEL'S HOUSE DIRECTLY AFTER SCHOOL AS THEY HAD PLANNED BECAUSE SHE HAD TO GO HOME AND GET THE FLAGPOLE FIRST. NOW WHAT COULD THEY WANT A FLAGPOLE FOR? THEY DON'T EVEN HAVE A FLAG. ARE THEY PLANNING TO PUT MY HEAD ON IT AFTERWARDS? I SAW THAT IN A BOOK ONCE. I BETTER GO OVER THERE AFTER SCHOOL AND SPY ON THEM. I KNOW A WAY TO GET THERE BY THE BACK FENCE. SOMETHING IS UP ALL RIGHT.

Math class droned on and Harriet used the time for thinking. Finally the bell rang and school was over. Everyone rushed to the door. Harriet followed behind, feeling slightly ridiculous. When they were outside everyone started off toward Rachel's house except Carrie, who went to her house. It was embarrassing. Harriet hid in the doorway until they were out of sight. As she stood there the rain stopped and the sun came out. She knew she should go there immediately, but it was time for her cake and milk. She stood for a minute, torn, but habit won.

She turned toward her house and ran as fast as she could. She could get it all over with fast and then sneak back there. The trees flew by as she ran, then the front door, then the steps down to the kitchen, and bang, she ran into the cook.

"This is too much. I'm going to quit if you do that one more time. Why can't you look where you're going? Do we have to put up traffic signals at the door? You're worse than those news trucks on the street. . . ." And so forth and so on, splutter, splutter, as she put the cake and milk on the table. Harriet took out her notebook and wrote:

THIS COOK CERTAINLY MAKES A LOT OF NOISE. MAYBE
WE COULD GET A QUIETER COOK. I CAN'T EVEN HEAR
MYSELF THINK. I HAVE TO PLAN BUT I CAN'T PLAN
UNTIL I KNOW <u>THEIR</u> PLAN. I BETTER GET GOING.

She slammed the book shut. The cook jumped.

"Why in the name of everything can't you do anything without all that noise? It's a simple enough thing
to close a book. It doesn't *have* to sound like an atomic
bomb. . . ." And so forth and so on. Her voice followed
Harriet all the way up to her room where she went to
put on her spy clothes.

First she went to the bathroom because she hadn't
in the morning, and when she was sitting there she
wrote in her notebook:

I LOVE MYSELF.

Then she got up and put on her spy clothes. When
she was all set she ran down the steps and out the
front door, banging it after her.

Rachel Hennessey lived on Eighty-fifth Street in a
ground-floor apartment in an old building. She and
her mother lived there alone because her father had
gone off somewhere. There was a big garden in back
and Harriet knew just how to get there by way of the
other gardens alongside.

On the corner of York and Eighty-fifth there was
a deserted old building about to be torn down, and
between this rotten old building and a new building
there was a little alley full of cats. Several old ladies
fed these cats, so there was a lot of tuna fish sitting
around in front of some makeshift houses they had
also made, which looked like beach cabanas for cats.

Harriet looked around and, seeing no one, climbed
over the iron railing in front of this alley. A cat with
one eye stared at her. She landed with a thump and

the cat with one eye hissed, backing away.

She ran to the back of the alley, her tools jangling. She climbed the fence and from there could see the whole stretch of the block of gardens. Rachel's was the fourth one over. Hoping that no one in the buildings would see her, or if they did they would keep their mouths shut, she began to climb fences and run through gardens until she came to the fence right next to Rachel's garden. Through a crack she could see and hear almost everything. She heard their voices, excited and screeching at each other, and saw a big piece of lumber rise up.

"Listen, Pinky, you're just stupid. This piece should go here, not over there." This was clearly Carrie Andrews talking.

Then Harriet saw the flagpole. It was a rather short flagpole, but it was a real one. At the top of it, fluttering against the blue sky, was a pair of purple socks.

Harriet stared at the socks. A dim feeling began to penetrate her. She didn't know what the feeling was until her heart began to beat fast, then she knew it was fear. Those socks made her afraid. If she could see what they were doing, maybe she wouldn't be afraid anymore.

"YOU'RE AN IDIOT!" Carrie Andrews to Pinky Whitehead.

"How can I build anything without a level?" Sport said to everyone in general.

Then Harriet found a hole and looked through. They were building a *house!* Incredible. But there they were. Everyone was rushing around with tools and wood and there was the semblance of a house emerging right in front of her. It leaned, of course. In fact the two back walls were the corner of the fence and it appeared to be pulling the fence down; but, never mind, it was a house.

Sport was in charge. He was telling everyone what

to do in a very irritated way. Carrie Andrews seemed to be the second in command. Except for about three pieces of new wood, the rest was old rotten wood from a chest they had broken up. The three new pieces didn't seem to bear any relation to each other. There were a couple of chairs being chopped up by Pinky right at that moment. Harriet scrunched closer to the fence to see better.

It was a funny scene. Carrie Andrews stood over Sport, yelling at the top of her lungs even though her mouth was right next to his ear. Sport was hammering a floor together. Laura Peters, Marion Hawthorne, and Rachel Hennessey were running around like fools. They had no idea how to do anything. Rachel tried to hammer and smashed her finger. After a while they got bored with trying and got into a conversation near Harriet's post. Janie joined them after an upright fell on her head.

"She's going to die when she finds out."

"Serves her right, mean thing."

"Boy, will she be jealous."

"She has delusions of grandeur anyway," said Janie, rubbing her head.

Harriet was puzzled. Who? Who were they talking about? She looked over and saw Beth Ellen in a corner by herself. What was she doing? She appeared to be drawing something on an old piece of wood. That was the one thing Beth Ellen could do, draw. But then Harriet looked more closely and saw that she wasn't exactly drawing, she was making letters on a sign in a very painstaking way.

Just at that moment the back door opened and Mrs. Hennessey called out, "Okay, kids, the cake is ready. Come and get it."

Homemade cake. Of course. That's why they had chosen Rachel's garden. Not everyone had a garden, but Janie did, and Beth Ellen did. Beth Ellen probably

174

wouldn't even give you an olive to eat over there. Once Harriet had spent the afternoon there and just to pass the time had looked in the refrigerator. There hadn't been anything but a jar of mayonnaise, a jar of artichoke hearts in olive oil, and some skimmed milk. Beth Ellen had agreed with her that it wasn't enough and had added that she felt hungry all the time because her nurse was on a diet and her grandmother was always out to dinner.

There was a mad scramble on the other side of the fence as they all ran to the back door and piled inside. Harriet felt lonely and rather hungry. She stood a minute thinking, then she went back through the gardens the way she had come. In the alley she noticed that there were seven cats sitting looking at her. One of them had no eyes at all. They all looked sick.

She climbed the iron railing and was back on the street. She sat on the nearest stoop and wrote down everything she had seen. When she finished she sat thinking for a minute. Then she opened her notebook and tore out a blank page from the back. She wanted to disguise her writing so she printed with her left hand:

Dear Mrs. Hennessey,
 All those kids hate Rachel. They just want your cake. Furthermore they will clutter up the backyard and also they constitute a nuisance.

        A Friend

Harriet looked quickly around. No one had seen her. She tucked her notebook away and walked hurriedly to Rachel's front door. Her heart beat fast as she walked up the steps and dropped a note in Mrs. Hennessey's mailbox. She thought she would burst she ran so fast down the steps and all the way to East End. She had never done anything like that before.

Would she be arrested? Sometimes on television people took notes to the police, but usually they had been thrown through a window with a rock. Maybe if you put it in the mailbox that didn't happen.

The next morning Harriet hurried to school. The night before it had occurred to her that maybe they just hadn't gotten around to asking her over that day. Maybe it had just been an oversight. It was a slim chance, but she preferred it to a nastier thought that had begun to creep around the edges of her mind.

When she went into her homeroom, she smiled at Laura Peters, who looked right back at her as though she weren't there. It made her feel creepy. Especially from Laura Peters, who smiled at everybody; who, in fact, smiled too much. Harriet sat down and wrote in her notebook in very small letters:

WHATEVER HAPPENS DON'T LET ME CRY

Just then Janie threw a spitball that hit her right in the face. Janie Gibbs? Janie had never thrown a spitball in her life. Janie Gibbs was above spitballs. And at me? she thought. At *me?* She remembered a poem she had read once, and she wrote it in her notebook.

IF YOU CAN KEEP YOUR HEAD WHEN ALL ABOUT YOU
ARE LOSING THEIRS AND BLAMING IT ON YOU

To write it down made her feel better. Miss Elson came in and they all stood up and said good morning. That made her feel better too. The world went on the same after all. The same things happened every morning. So *what* if they didn't like her? *She* would go on the same. *She* was Harriet M. Welsch, and she would continue to be Harriet M. Welsch, and that was the thing to remember. She chose a clean sheet of paper and wrote Harriet M. Welsch at the top. It looked reassuringly important.

As she was looking at it, with just a trace of a satisfied smile on her face, an incident happened. Rachel Hennessey passed her desk carrying a bottle of ink. It happened so fast that it was impossible to tell anything, but somehow she fell toward Harriet and a stain of spreading, running blue ink went over the Harriet M. Welsch, making it disappear, and continued toward Harriet, as she watched in horror, spilling down all over her dress, down the front even onto her legs and into her shoes and socks.

Rachel started fluttering and saying "Oh, Miss Elson, oh, Miss Elson, look what has happened!" in a voice that wasn't at all her own but sounded, in fact, like her mother's. All the kids jumped up and Miss Elson came running. Harriet sat despondently, blue all over. She had grabbed at the bottle, so now she had blue ink on both hands and up her arms. Every time she moved, her arms flung spots of ink onto everyone, onto Pinky's white shirt, onto Miss Elson's nose.

Everyone backed away, and Miss Elson said "Oh, Harriet" as though Harriet had done it. Harriet felt sodden. She sat there in her ink and didn't move.

"Now, dear, it's not so bad. You must simply run home and take a bath and change. You'll be back in time for math class. Rachel, that was incredibly clumsy. Sport, run to the bathroom and get some paper towels. We'll have to wipe all this up. Pinky, run with him, bring the whole roll. My heavens, this *is* a mess, isn't it?"

There was a great deal of fuss. The interesting thing was how Rachel, Laura, Pinky, Janie, Marion, all of them cooed over Harriet when Miss Elson was watching. They helped her out of the seat, saying nice things the whole time. Then when Miss Elson went to the door to grab the paper roll from Pinky, Marion poured the rest of the ink down Harriet's back. At this, Harriet turned and hit Marion across the face, making Marion's face entirely blue.

"Now, now, Harriet, we mustn't blame others for our own trouble. That's no way to behave. Rachel couldn't help it and Marion had nothing to do with it. It simply was an accident, and I'm sure Rachel feels terrible about it."

"Oh, yes, Miss Elson, I do," Rachel piped up hurriedly.

"That's right. Now, you see, Harriet? When people hurt us they are sorry afterward, and we have to forgive them quickly so they will feel better." Miss Elson huffed and puffed.

Rachel was laughing so hard behind Miss Elson's back that she was almost caught when Miss Elson turned to extend her blue arm to pull Rachel toward Harriet. "No, Rachel must know that she couldn't help what she did and you must know that too, Harriet." Harriet shot two steely eyes in Rachel's direction. Rachel smiled like an angel.

"I'm *terribly* sorry, Harriet. I must have tripped. I *really* am *sorry*." Her eyes were shining so much that Harriet knew she was one minute from falling on the floor in helpless laughter. Harriet threw her a contemptuous glance and looked down at her blue legs. Pinky and Sport were scrubbing away, one on each leg, as Miss Elson tried to squeeze some of the ink out of the dress into a small cup.

Suddenly Harriet couldn't stand it anymore. She grabbed her notebook and wrenched herself away from them all, flinging ink all over everyone as she did.

She catapulted herself out of the door. She could hear their little flurries and shouts dimly behind her as she ran down the big steps, her feet making slush,

178

slush noises in her ink-filled shoes. The school porter put out his arms to stop her as she went by and got a blob of ink in his eye for his trouble. She ran even faster out on the street because everyone stared at her. I'm the blue monster of East End Avenue, she thought as she careened across Eighty-sixth Street and up the block to her house.

She was still leaving tracks as she entered her house, so she knew there would be spots on the rug but she didn't care. The important thing was to get upstairs before anyone saw her. Her room reached at last, she fled into the bathroom and locked the door. There she began frantically to peel off all her clothes while the tears, finally come, welled forth as hot as tiny knives down her cheeks. She began to run the bath water, almost unable to see the taps.

There was a knock on the door and the cook's voice came through. "What's the matter? What you doing home? You taking a bath in there?"

"Yes," Harriet managed to say, composing herself.

"What you doing taking a bath when you supposed

to be in school? Your mama's not here. I'm all alone here. What am I supposed to do about you?"

"They sent me home to take a bath. It's all right. Go away."

"Who you saying 'go away' to? Don't you tell me to go away. I don't see what's all right about it. I never heard of any child coming home middle of the day to take a bath."

"Well, now you've heard it. The teacher SENT me home."

There was a thick silence. *"Hhrumph"* came through the door. She could almost hear the cook thinking. Finally, "You not hurt, are you?"

Harriet sighed. "No, I'm not hurt." There was another silence, then Harriet said, "Can I have my lunch here?"

"You already took one tomato sandwich this morning."

"I forgot it."

"The work in this house is too much. Take your bath and come downstairs. I'll make another sandwich."

"TOMATO," Harriet shouted.

"I know, tomato, tomato. I'll be glad if I never see another tomato." And she shuffled away.

Harriet sighed with relief. She put one toe in the water, immediately staining the whole tub blue. Then she lowered herself by stages into the hot tub, there to cry softly for a long time before she could bathe.

The next afternoon after school Harriet went stealthily over the fences again to watch. There had been no more incidents in school that day except for the fact that no one would sit with her at lunch again and no one spoke to her. She was getting used to it in a way, but then, she thought, there wasn't much else she could do.

180

As she peeked through the Hennesseys' fence, she could see that they had done quite a bit after the cake the other day. The whole structure of a little house was up except for a little to be done around the door. Beth Ellen was still working on the sign. Sport was organizing everyone to look through the remaining lumber for two nice pieces to form the sides of the door. Rachel suddenly spoke up. "My mother got a note in the mailbox yesterday. She says it was from some crank, but I saw it and I think its from *that spy.*"

"What did it say?" Carrie asked.

Rachel spoke importantly, "Oh, it was just ridiculous—said nobody liked me, they only liked the cake."

There was a small silence.

Pinky, who was hammering, said thoughtfully, "Well, it's *very* good *cake.*"

Harriet laughed to herself. Pinky always said something dumb.

Janie said, "Oh, Pinky."

Marion said, "I bet it *was* from her because that's what *she* said about Rachel in that book of hers."

Rachel hurried on as though she hadn't heard anything. "It said a lot of things about us making a nuisance and so forth, but really it sounded just like *her.* I'm sure it was her."

Beth Ellen got up suddenly and squeaked, "I'm finished. I'm finished." They all hurried over and exclaimed a long time about how beautiful the sign was, what a good job Beth Ellen had done, and all that sort of thing. Beth Ellen stood and grinned wildly as though she'd just done the Sistine Chapel. I bet you, Harriet thought, that's the first time anybody ever said anything nice to her.

Pinky said, "Is it dry?"

"Almost," said Beth Ellen.

Sport leaned down and said, "If I pick it up by the edges, I think I can hang it up. It just needs to be nailed in over the door." He picked it up and carried it across the yard. As he was changing it from hand to hand to put it in position the face of it was turned toward Harriet and she saw with amazement that it read:

THE SPY CATCHER CLUB

The lettering was very bad, but then what else would Beth Ellen do? Harriet sat down with a *plump* on the damp ground. So it was she, Harriet, that they were talking about. She was *her*. How odd, she thought, to think of yourself as *her*. She took out her notebook and wrote:

THEY HAVE A CLUB AND I AM NOT IN IT. IT IS ALSO A CLUB AGAINST ME. THEY ARE REALLY OUT TO GET ME. I HAVE NEVER HAD TO GO THROUGH SOMETHING LIKE THIS. I WILL HAVE TO BE VERY BRAVE. I WILL NEVER GIVE UP THIS NOTEBOOK BUT IT IS CLEAR THAT THEY ARE GOING TO BE AS MEAN AS THEY CAN UNTIL I DO. THEY JUST DON'T KNOW HARRIET M. WELSCH.

Harriet got up, walked solidly to the fence, and climbed noisily over. She didn't even care if they heard her now. She knew what she had to do and she was going to do it.

CHAPTER 12

The next morning she arrived very early at school and was writing furiously in the notebook when they all filed in. They had been chattering excitedly among themselves, but they all stopped when they saw her. She continued to write with renewed zeal until Miss Elson came in. She stood up with the others but then sat down and wrote some more. When Miss Elson handed back the test papers from the day before she didn't look up but just continued writing. Every now and then she would glance meaningfully at one of the others to let them know that *At that very moment* she was writing about THAT PERSON. They all watched her nervously. Actually she was doing nothing of the kind. She had begun to write a series of memories starting with the first thing she could remember at all, which was standing up in her crib, looking out the window at the park, and shouting with every ounce of breath in her body. She was writing a later memory:

I REMEMBER WHEN WE LIVED AT SEVENTY-SEVENTH AND FIFTH. I HAD TO RIDE THE SCHOOL BUS EVERY DAY

INSTEAD OF WALKING. THERE WAS A VERY NASTY BOY WHO LIVED IN THE NEXT APARTMENT. I WAS SEVEN AND HE WAS THREE. HIS NAME WAS CARTER WINGFELD AND HE BURPED ALL THE TIME. HE WAS SO NASTY-LOOKING THAT I PINCHED HIM ONCE WHEN HIS MOTHER WASN'T LOOKING. MY MOTHER DIDN'T KNOW IT WAS ME THAT PINCHED HIM BUT OLE GOLLY KNEW AND SHE LET ME HAVE IT GOOD FOR THAT. SHE SAID EVEN IF HE WAS THE NASTIEST THING I EVER SAW IN MY LIFE I SHOULD JUST THINK ABOUT THAT TO MYSELF AND NOT DO ANYTHING TO HIM BECAUSE HE COULDN'T HELP HIS NASTINESS.

She looked around the room. Apprehensive glances came her way now and then; otherwise nothing was happening. She wrote:

CAN THEY HELP WHAT THEY'RE DOING? I WISH I KNEW WHAT OLE GOLLY WOULD THINK OF THIS. I HAVE TO KNOW WHAT SHE THINKS. HOW CAN I FIND OUT? I THINK SHE WOULD SAY THAT THEY COULD BECAUSE THEY'RE TRYING TO CONTROL ME AND MAKE ME GIVE UP THIS NOTEBOOK, AND SHE ALWAYS SAID THAT PEOPLE WHO TRY TO CONTROL PEOPLE AND CHANGE PEOPLE'S HABITS ARE THE ONES THAT MAKE ALL THE TROUBLE. IF YOU DON'T LIKE SOMEBODY, WALK AWAY, SHE SAID, BUT DON'T TRY AND MAKE THEM LIKE YOU. I THINK SHE WOULD HATE THIS WHOLE THING.

She looked up and saw everyone starting his work. She took out a piece of paper, feeling listless and bored as she did. She started to write her name at the top of the page, but it didn't seem like any fun. She looked around at everyone. Most people weren't looking at her, but the ones who were, Marion and Rachel in particular, had nasty looks on their faces. She looked back at the paper, gave up trying to take an interest in her own name, and went back to writing in her notebook. Miss Elson's harsh voice finally reached her, "Harriet, you're not paying attention." Harriet looked up and saw everyone looking at her with contempt. They're thinking, Just what you'd expect of her, she thought to herself. She put the notebook under the desk on her knees where Miss Elson couldn't see it. Whenever Miss Elson turned to the blackboard Harriet looked under and wrote a little.

THAT PINKY WHITEHEAD IS THE MOST DISGUSTING THING I EVER SAW. WHAT MUST HIS MOTHER HAVE THOUGHT THE FIRST TIME SHE LOOKED AT HIM? SHE MUST HAVE THROWN UP.

During math class she wrote all the time. Everyone was bent over their work and Miss Harris, the math teacher, was too old to get up and walk around and look. Harriet got so involved she didn't even think where she was. She didn't, in fact, even hear the bell. From away far away she heard someone saying "Harriet—oh, Harriet" and then "Harriet Welsch" suddenly very loudly. She almost fell off the chair. She looked up and the room was empty except for old Miss Harris who was looking at her with the meanest look she had ever seen on a teacher. Harriet stared back at her, terrified.

Miss Harris stood up. "It's time to go home, Harriet, but before you go I think you had better show me what has kept you so entranced during math class." She advanced slowly toward Harriet. Harriet could see her bony, clawlike hand covered with brown spots reaching . . . *reaching* . . .

Harriet got up so fast she knocked her chair over. She caught sight of Miss Harris reeling backward away from her as she made such a great leap for the door she might have been pole vaulting. Miss Harris gasped and her hand flew to her throat, but Harriet was out and gone, hugging her notebook, running for her life.

The next day was even worse. She didn't even make any pretense of doing her work. She just wrote all the time. Miss Elson spoke to her four times and Miss Harris yelled three times, then gave up. At the end of the day she went straight home, had her cake and milk, then took her notebook over to the park and sat on a bench. She found that she enjoyed writing under the trees.

I HAVE HEARD THAT PIGEONS MAKE PEOPLE GET CANCER SO I WILL STAY AWAY FROM THEM. ON THE OTHER HAND THEY ARE PRETTY. I LIKE TO LOOK AT THE MAYOR'S HOUSE. IT IS A NICE WHITE HOUSE. ONCE MY DADDY TOLD ME THAT THERE WAS A LOT OF HOUSES LIKE THAT ALL UP AND DOWN THE RIVER HERE BUT THEN THEY MADE A PARK AND THREW AWAY ALL THE HOUSES. THEY SHOULD HAVE LEFT SOME OLD HAUNTED ONES FOR CHILDREN TO GO AND PLAY IN. I WOULD HAVE LOCKED PINKY IN THE BASEMENT UNTIL HIS HAIR TURNED WHITE.

I LIKE THE TUGBOATS. I DON'T HAVE ANYONE TO PLAY WITH. I DON'T EVEN HAVE ANYONE TO TALK TO NOW THEY GOT RID OF OLE GOLLY. I AM GOING TO FINISH UP THESE MEMOIRS AND SELL THEM TO THE BOOK OF THE MONTH SELECTION THEN MY MOTHER WILL GET THE BOOK IN THE MAIL AS A SURPRISE. THEN I WILL BE SO RICH AND FAMOUS THAT PEOPLE WILL BOW IN THE STREETS AND SAY THERE GOES HARRIET M. WELSCH— SHE IS VERY FAMOUS YOU KNOW. RACHEL HENNESSEY WILL PLOTZ.

Harriet looked up when she heard the toot-toot of a

toy whistle. She raised her eyebrows at what she saw.

They were making a parade along the river. The Boy with the Purple Socks, now wearing green socks, walked in front carrying the flagpole with the purple socks attached. There was a rat-a-tat-tat from a toy drum that Pinky Whitehead was beating, and behind them there was a squadron formed by Rachel Hennessey, Marion Hawthorne, Carrie Andrews, Laura Peters, Beth Ellen, and Sport and Janie. They marched in formation like a platoon, and when they turned, Harriet could see a sign attached to Beth Ellen's back which said:

THIS PARADE
THE COURTESY OF
THE SPY CATCHER CLUB

Harriet sat frozen, watching them march up and down. She was afraid to move because they might see her. Her worst fears were realized a moment later when Marion Hawthorne gave a big blast on the whistle and gestured frantically. Nine heads turned in Harriet's direction. Harriet stiffened. They were going to march *right past her*.

They turned into the lane sedately. Harriet didn't know what to do. She felt that if she showed any reaction at all it would please them too much. On the other hand, if she showed no reaction at all when a whole parade was marching right under her nose they would know they had affected her.

She sat stiffly on her bench. It was horribly embarrassing. It seemed to take about an hour for them to come toward her and then they were passing in front of her. As they went past she felt like General Eisenhower reviewing the troops. It took everything she had not to salute.

When they got close she saw that The Boy with the Purple Socks wore a sign around his neck which said:

ASK TO BE TOLD
THE LEGEND OF THE PURPLE SOCKS
10 CENTS

When they were directly opposite her they all stuck their tongues out in unison as though they had practiced, and Pinky gave an extra little roll to the drum.

They marched away. Would they come back around? Harriet opened her notebook:

WELL, THAT'S NOT MY FAULT. I NEVER TOLD HIM TO WEAR OR NOT WEAR PURPLE SOCKS. HE SHOULD HAVE KEPT ON WEARING PURPLE SOCKS. SOME PEOPLE ACT LIKE A MARTYR AT THE DROP OF A HAT, OR A SOCK, HA HA. I HEAR THEM COMING BACK. I THINK I WILL GO HOME.

Harriet walked casually away from the bench. When she saw they were coming around again, she dove under a bush until they marched past. Then she went home, went up to her room, and closed the door.

WELL, I JUST WON'T GO TO THE PARK ANYMORE. THAT'S NOTHING. WHO WANTS TO GO THERE IF IT'S FULL OF IDIOTS WALKING AROUND IN PARADES. I CAN WRITE IN MY NOTEBOOK JUST AS WELL SITTING ON MY BED. I DON'T CARE ABOUT THEIR DUMB OLD CLUB ANYWAY IF ALL THEY'RE GOING TO DO IS MARCH AROUND A LOT.

There was a knock on the door, and when Harriet said, "What?" her mother entered.

"Harriet, I've got to talk to you. I've just come back from your school. Miss Elson called me up this afternoon and said that I had better come over and have a talk about you."

Harriet's throat closed up.

"There's nothing to be afraid of. She just wanted to talk about your school work. She says that for the last week you haven't done any at all. What about it?"

"I haven't anything to say."

"What do you mean? Did you do your work or not?"

"No. I don't think so. I can't remember."

"Harriet, these are very unsatisfactory answers. Is something else bothering you?"

"No."

Harriet's mother pulled the chair over to the bed, sat down, and stared at Harriet. "What have you got there?"

"What?" Harriet looked around innocently.

"You know perfectly well what. Is that the same notebook?"

"No, a different one."

"You *know* what I *mean,* Harriet. Are you still writing down mean things about people?"

"No. I'm writing my memoirs."

Her mother, for some reason or other, laughed. She then smiled warmly at Harriet. "Both Miss Elson and Miss Harris say that you do nothing whatever anymore but write in that notebook. Is that right?"

"Yes."

"They say that I must take it away from you or you will never learn anything."

"I'm learning plenty."

"What are you learning?"

"Everything about everybody."

Mrs. Welsch consulted a small slip of paper. "History, Geography, French, Science—all bad. You're even doing badly in English. And we *know* you can't add and subtract."

Harriet just sat there. School seemed a million miles away, a moon that she had been to once.

"I'm afraid that you're only going to be able to play with this notebook after school, but not during school hours."

"I'm not *playing*. Who says I'm *playing?* I'm WORKING!"

"Look, dear, at the moment you're in school, so your work is school. Just like your father works at the office, you work at school. School work is your work."

"What do *you* do?"

"A lot of unseen, unappreciated things. That's not the point. At the moment your work is going to school and learning, and you're not doing that. Now you can have the notebook as soon as you come home from school. I'll give it to the cook and you can have it just as soon as you come in."

"No," said Harriet.

"Yes. Now that's definite."

"I'll throw a tantrum."

"So throw, but I'm not going to stand here and watch you. Now in the morning I don't want to see you leaving here with any notebook, nor are you to arrive at school with one. Miss Elson is going to check."

Harriet lay flat on her stomach on the bed. She pushed her face into the pillow.

"Honey, is something bothering you?"

"No" came out very muffled.

CHAPTER 13

The next morning Harriet was frisked by her mother. The notebook was taken away and given to the cook, who looked as though she might eat it.

Harriet walked sadly to school. She dragged her feet and looked intently at the cracks in the cement. She dragged in the door, up the steps, and into her homeroom. She sat down and stared at the floor, not hearing anything around her.

After Miss Elson had come in and they had said good morning to her, she went immediately to Harriet, made her stand up to be searched, then searched her desk. Harriet submitted limply. When no notebook was found, Miss Elson patted Harriet on the head like a good puppy and went back to her desk in the front.

Some very interested eyes watched this whole procedure. When it was finished everyone snickered. They whispered a lot and stared at Harriet, who stared at the floor.

Harriet did her work. She didn't care anymore about signing her name, and she got no pleasure from the work she did, but she did it. Everything bored her.

She found that when she didn't have a notebook it was hard for her to think. The thoughts came slowly, as though they had to squeeze through a tiny door to get to her, whereas when she wrote, they flowed out faster than she could put them down. She sat very stupidly with a blank mind until finally "I feel different" came slowly into her head. She sat digesting the thought like a Thanksgiving dinner.

Yes, she thought, after a long pause. And then, after more time, Mean, I feel mean.

She looked around with a mean look for everyone. Nobody saw her. She felt her face contorting. It was an impressive moment that everyone missed. It was a moment that Harriet would never forget.

When the bell rang for lunch, it was as though she didn't have to think anymore. Everything happened as though she had planned it but she really hadn't. For example, when the bell rang Pinky Whitehead jumped up and ran down the aisle. Harriet put her foot out and he fell flat on his face.

A terrific wail went up from his prone body, and when he raised his face his nose was bleeding. Harriet looked extremely blank. Inside she felt a sense of very personal satisfaction.

She got up and walked quietly out, stepping delicately over Pinky's writhing body. She knew no one would ever think of her because she had never done anything like that in her life. She went and got her tomato sandwich.

During lunch she sat, owl-eyed, by herself. She felt her thoughts limping like crippled children. When the bell rang again, she rose like a robot and walked to the door.

She was pushed helplessly into the crush at the door. Carrie Andrews was right in front of her. Without thought, Harriet pinched her expertly on the leg. Carrie let out a terrible scream and looked around with a wild red flush on her face.

Harriet looked solidly ahead. No one would think of her because she had never pinched anyone in her life. Carrie Andrews, as a matter of fact, sometimes pinched, but the only one really *known* for pinching was Marion Hawthorne. Carrie leaned over and hit Marion in the head, even though Marion was four people away and couldn't possibly have pinched her. A large fight started, and Harriet squeezed her way out and into math class.

She sat, looking Miss Harris forlornly in the eye while the others filed in. Miss Harris, after making certain Harriet had no notebook, tried to smile warmly at her, but Harriet looked away.

Without a notebook there was nothing to do but listen to Miss Harris. Having never done this before, Harriet was totally lost. Miss Harris went on and on about some bridge. Everyone copied down a lot of numbers. Harriet copied them down too but they made absolutely no sense. They went from there into a spirited discussion about buying and selling a lot of lamb chops.

Harriet wadded up a piece of paper and, again without thought, sent it flying into Sport's ear. Sport gave a little yelp but recovered quickly. At his next opportunity he looked around. Harriet shot him a mean look. He stared at her a minute, his eyes wide with a growing perplexity and fear. Then he looked away quickly.

There was in process an incomprehensible discussion about boats and how many knots they went. Harriet tried to think, but it was impossible. She quite abruptly threw a pencil straight into Beth Ellen's face.

Beth Ellen looked horrorstruck, and when she saw Harriet looking at her, burst into loud ridiculous baby tears.

The bell rang, and as Miss Harris scuttled over to Beth Ellen, Harriet walked to the door and down the

steps. She ran home, into her house, down the steps, and bang, right into the cook.

"How can you do it every day? Do they aim you from school right at me?"

"Give me my notebook, please."

"What notebook?"

"Whatdya mean? My NOTEBOOK. My NOTE-BOOK!" Harriet had a moment of sheer panic.

"Listen to me, you apologize for almost knocking me to the floor." The cook stood, hands on hips, as though she had all the time in the world.

"I apologize."

"All right." She turned her back in a grumpy way and stuck her hands back into the dishwater.

"My NOTEBOOK," Harriet shouted.

"Oh, all right, all right. Can't you wait just one

minute till I get this soap off my hands?"

"No, no, no, I can't wait. I want it NOW."

"All right. All right." She washed her hands, dried them, and reached down under the sink. From way back in the back she pulled out the notebook with a little cleanser spilled on it.

Harriet grabbed it and ran out of the room.

"Hey, how about your cake and milk?"

Harriet didn't even hear. She ran into her room and flung herself on the bed. She lay quietly for a minute looking reverently at her notebook and then opened it. She had had an unreasonable fear that it would be empty, but there was her handwriting, reassuring if not beautiful. She grabbed up the pen and felt the mercy of her thoughts coming quickly, zooming through her head out the pen onto the paper. What a relief, she thought to herself; for a moment I thought I had dried up. She wrote a lot about what she felt, relishing the joy of her fingers gliding across the page, the sheer relief of communication. After a while she sat back and began to really think hard. Then she wrote again:

SOMETHING IS DEFINITELY HAPPENING TO ME. I AM CHANGING. I DON'T FEEL LIKE ME AT ALL. I DON'T EVER LAUGH OR THINK ANYTHING FUNNY. I JUST FEEL MEAN ALL OVER. I WOULD LIKE TO HURT EACH ONE OF THEM IN A SPECIAL WAY THAT WOULD HURT ONLY THEM.

And then she made a list:

MARION HAWTHORNE: FROGS. PUT ONE IN HER DESK. A SNAKE WOULD BE BETTER.
RACHEL HENNESSEY: HER FATHER. ASK HER WHERE HE WENT.
LAURA PETERS: HER HAIR. CUT IT OFF. OR MAKE A BALD SPOT.

PINKY WHITEHEAD: MEAN LOOKS. THAT'S ALL HE
  NEEDS.
CARRIE ANDREWS: TELL HER FATHER SOMETHING
  TERRIBLE ABOUT HER WHICH IS A LIE.
BETH ELLEN HANSEN: HATES TO BE HIT. HIT HER.
JANIE: BREAK HER LITTLE FINGER.
SPORT: CALL HIM A SISSY AND TELL EVERYONE HE READS
  COOK BOOKS.
BOY WITH PURPLE SOCKS: ??

She couldn't think of anything for him because he
was so dull. Well, she thought, I will watch him tomorrow.

The next day at school Harriet concentrated on
these things. She thought about them so hard she didn't
do her work at all. The only words she spoke all day
were when she asked Rachel Hennessey why she didn't
have a father living in the house. Actually what she
said was, "You don't have a father, do you, Rachel?"
in a fairly conversational tone.

Rachel looked at her, horrified, and yelled, "I do
TOO."

Harriet said briskly, "Oh, no, you don't."

"I do too," Rachel shouted.

"Well, he doesn't love you."

"He does too."

"Well, then why doesn't he live with you?"

And Rachel burst into tears.

The next day she went to the park immediately
after breakfast. She looked for a long time in the bush-
es and finally found a frog. It was a very small frog,
maybe a baby. She picked him up very carefully so
as not to squash him and put him in the pocket of her
jumper. Then she ran to school, keeping her hand

lightly around him so he couldn't jump out. She ran to her homeroom and lifted the top of Marion Hawthorne's desk. Then she carefully put the frog down inside. The frog hopped once and stared up at her peevishly. She stared back at him. She had grown rather fond of him. She hoped nothing happened to him in the confusion.

She closed the desk softly so as not to frighten him, then sat down primly in her place. The children all came in. While they were standing up saying good morning Harriet grabbed a chunk of Laura Peters' hair and chopped it off with some scissors she had ready. Laura Peters didn't feel a thing. She sat down quite happily, never suspecting that she had a large chunk cut out of her hair. Harriet stared at the spot with a kind of joy.

Just as Sport, who had seen the whole thing, was about to rat, Marion Hawthorne opened her desk.

Harriet had never seen such confusion or heard such screams in her life. It was extremely gratifying. It was as though the whole class erupted in a volcanic shower of cries, running, yelps, and tumbling bodies. No one at first knew what had happened. Marion screamed so loudly that everyone jumped up. Then, when they saw what appeared to be a small brown spot leaping from desk to desk, onto a child's shoulder, onto another desk, from there to an arm, they lost their heads completely without being able to tell what about. In the confusion Harriet got up quietly and walked home.

When she came in, the cook said in a very quiet voice, "What are you doing? You're not supposed to be home?"

"I'm just home."

"But why are you home?" the cook said ever so softly.

"Why are you whispering?" shouted Harriet.

"I have a new cake in the oven," whispered the cook. "It will be ready in a minute. You mustn't bounce around, or walk heavy, or shout, because it will fall."

Harriet stood there. She munched a thought over in her mind. Without warning she ran to the center of the room, overturned a chair, then jumped up and down, stomping her feet with all her might.

The cook screamed one long scream and flew to the oven. "Look what you've done, you terrible child. That does it. I quit. If I have to put up with you one more day I will go stark raving yelling crazy, and it's not worth it for what I get paid."

Harriet left the room.

The cook stood looking at the flat cake. It lay there in the pan as if someone had stepped on it. "There is something wrong in this house. It was never this bad before. Mrs. Welsch is going to hear from me all right, all right."

Harriet lay upstairs in her room all day. She didn't look out the window or read or write in her notebook. She just lay there looking at the ceiling. Through her mind rang one single name endlessly—Ole Golly, Ole Golly, Ole Golly, Ole Golly—as though saying it would make her appear.

In the late afternoon she could hear the cook yelling at her mother. "I'm quitting, I tell you. I'm tired of being run into every day, and being screamed at, and now she's stomped my cake and that does it."

"Oh, please, don't leave us now. We NEED you," Harriet's mother was almost begging.

"I wouldn't stay for all the money in the world. I'm leaving right now."

"How about a five dollar raise? I think we could see our way clear . . ."

"Something better be done about that Harriet. I

hate to leave you in the lurch, but she run into me one more time or pull a nasty trick like stomping my cake and that's it."

"I understand."

"I'm a COOK. I'm not a NURSE."

Harriet in her room thought, Ole Golly, Ole Golly, Ole Golly.

"Of course, I understand completely."

Cook retired loudly to the kitchen, and Harriet's mother came up the steps. Harriet could hear her coming. She kept looking at the ceiling. There was a pattern there made by the leaves of a tree outside the window, a very interesting pattern which changed over and over.

"Harriet, what is the matter with you?" Her mother stood in the doorway. Harriet didn't answer and inside the song went, Ole Golly, please, please, Ole Golly.

"Harriet, do you know what my day has been like? I had a frantic call at the hairdresser's to come to your school immediately. I went over there and heard how you had spent your morning. That Laura Peters is practically going to have to have her head shaved. Marion Hawthorne went home sick and Miss Elson was on the verge of tears, she was so wrought up. She'll probably never get over it. She says it was bedlam for hours. Then I come home to find the cook quitting. Well, luckily I saved that situation, but, Harriet, this has gone too far. Now you're going to have to sit up and talk to me. What do you think you're doing?"

Harriet didn't move. Inside the song had stopped and she felt a dim sense of pleasure side by side with a swelling current of fear.

"Harriet?"

She lay there.

Her mother turned and left the room, saying as she went, "Your father will be home in an hour. If you're

not talking to me by then you'll have to talk to him."
Harriet lay there the rest of the afternoon watching the
leaf pattern change and fade. She heard her father
come in.

"I just can't cope with this kind of thing. I come
home from the office and I want some peace and
quiet and a martini. I come home tonight and the ice
bucket isn't even filled, you are practically raving, I
can hear that fink of a cook all the way from the
kitchen—she is yelling so loud—and you tell me you
just gave her a five dollar raise. Now make sense,
woman!"

There was a lot of mumbling and then a door closed.
Her mother had taken her father into the library. Everyone always went into the library to be fussed at.

She lay in the dark and stared at nothing. She didn't
blame her father for being angry. It was all so boring.
When she closed her eyes sometimes she saw a yellow
spot. She almost fell asleep. A slant of light fell across
her face and she opened one eye a crack, to see her
father standing in the doorway. She closed her eyes.

"Harriet, are you asleep?"

Harriet didn't move.

"Harriet, answer me."

Harriet just lay there, scarcely breathing.

"Listen, I know perfectly well you're not asleep. I
used to do the same thing to *my* father. So you just sit
up and talk to me."

Quickly Harriet sat up, leaned over, and in one
perfectly coordinated motion threw a shoe at her father.

"Well . . . of all the splutter splutter. Something has
to be done. . . . This child—come in here. I think we'd
better call . . . What the—" The door banged shut.

Harriet lay there as though she had never moved,
had never thrown a shoe, had never been unhappy,
had never caught a frog. She thought quietly, Wait

until I break Janie's finger. Then she fell asleep quite suddenly. Late at night she awoke to feel her mother putting her pajamas on her and tucking her in. She slept blissfully.

CHAPTER 14

When Harriet got up the next morning she was starving because she hadn't had any dinner the night before. She went downstairs in her pajamas and sat down at the breakfast table.

"Harriet, go back up and put on your clothes."

"No."

"What do you mean 'no'?" Her mother stared at her wide-eyed.

"NO. That's all, just no."

"Get up those steps this minute," her father said, "or you'll get a whaling you'll never forget."

Harriet went back up and put on her clothes. She came back and sat down again. Neither of her parents had a paper in front of them, and they seemed to look at her a lot.

"Did you wash?"

"No."

"Then go back and wash."

"No."

"Harriet, you always go back and wash."

Silence.

"Harriet, go up and wash."

"No."

Her father looked at her mother. "We are doing this none too soon, I see. But before we all get a lot of newfangled ideas, may I say, Harriet, that you are going to go upstairs right this minute and wash or you won't be able to sit down for a week."

Harriet went back upstairs and washed. Somehow it all made her feel rather pleasant and she hummed a little coming back down.

"This morning," her mother said, "you are not going to school."

"I know it."

"How do you know it? Harriet, were you spying?"

"No."

"Then how did you know?"

"I decided I wasn't going. I don't like school anymore."

"Oh, well, that's not exactly what I meant. I meant that this morning you are going with me to pay a visit to someone."

Harriet's heart leaped. "Ole Golly? Is Ole Golly in town?"

Her mother and father exchanged a glance. "No," said her mother, "we're going to see a doctor."

"Oh." Harriet chewed some bacon. "Dr. Andrews?" she asked casually, planning to spread some rumor about Carrie when she was in the office.

"No," said her mother and looked rather helplessly at her father. Her father went *"Hhrrumph"* and cleared his throat a couple of times. Then he said, "This is a rather pleasant chap you're going to see. He's not a fink like most doctors."

Harriet kept eating without looking at him. Maybe, she thought, I could just say my father thinks Dr. Andrews is a fink and that would be enough for Carrie.

When she was finished she went outside to wait for her mother. She looked in the direction of her school and could see all the children piling in the door. She didn't care if she ever went in there again. It seemed a hundred years ago that she had liked to write Harriet M. Welsch at the top of the page.

Her mother finally came around in the car and Harriet got in. Her mother drove over to Ninety-sixth and Fifth, then three times around the block looking for a parking place, and finally put the car in a garage, fuming in rage the whole time.

In the elevator Harriet said suddenly, "What am I coming here for? I don't feel sick." Although she felt a little sick as she said it.

"You just talk to this doctor. He doesn't do anything to you."

"But I don't know him."

"That's all right. He's a nice man."

"But what do I talk about?"

"Anything he wants to."

They got to the seventh floor and her mother buzzed the buzzer on a blue door. It was answered almost immediately by the funniest-looking man Harriet had ever seen. He had bright red hair that stood straight up behind a bald crown, an enormous mouth grinning with yellow teeth, funny glasses with big black rims, and he was very, very tall—so tall he bent over a little. He also, she noticed, had a *very* strange nose and very long feet.

"Hello, there," he said cheerfully.

Harriet sneered at him. She hated people who tried to make you like them right away.

"Hello, Dr. Wagner. This is Harriet."

Harriet looked away. She felt stupid standing there. They were both looking at her.

"Well, now, won't you come into my office and we'll have a little talk."

The library all over again, thought Harriet; this is a long way to come to be fussed at. Her mother smiled at her, then went into the waiting room while Harriet followed the red hair into its office. The office was large with a sky-blue rug, a couch, and for some reason, a spinet. Harriet stood stock-still in the middle of the room as Dr. Wagner sat down in one of the two huge armchairs.

He looked at her pleasantly, rather expectantly, and she looked back. There was a great deal of silence.

"Well?" said Harriet after a long time.

"Well, what?" he said pleasantly.

"Well, what do we do now?"

"You can do anything you like."

"Can I leave?"

"Do you want to?"

"Well, what am I SUPPOSED to do?" Harriet was getting quite angry.

Dr. Wagner scratched his nose, "Well, let's see. We could play a game. Do you like games?"

This was the dumbest thing Harriet had ever heard of. To come all this way to play a game. She bet her mother didn't know this. What was the matter with this man? She decided that the only nice thing to do would be to play along with him, for a while. "Yeah . . . I like games . . . all right."

"What kind of games?"

Oh, what a tiresome man. "Any old game. You're the one wanted to play a game."

"Do you play chess?"

"No." Ole Golly was going to teach me, she thought, but she never got around to it.

"Well, how about Monopoly?"

Just about the most boring game in the world. It had everything in it that Harriet hated. "Okay, if you want to."

Dr. Wagner got up and went to a cabinet next to the door. When he opened it Harriet could see all sorts of games, dolls, doll houses, and trucks. She tried to be nice about it, but she was curious. "Do you sit here all day playing with all those things?" Wait till her mother got a load of this.

He looked at her archly, "What do you think?"

"Whadya mean, what do I think?"

"Do you think I sit here all day playing with these toys?"

"How do I know? You got a whole closet full of 'em."

"Don't you have toys at home?"

This was too much. "Yes," she shouted, "but I'm eleven."

"Oh." He looked somewhat taken aback, standing there with the Monopoly board in his hand.

Harriet began to feel sorry for him. "Well," she said, "shall we play one game?"

He looked relieved. He set up the board carefully on the coffee table. Then he went to the desk drawer and got out a notebook and a pen. Then he sat down across from her.

Harriet stared at the notebook. "What's that?"

"A notebook."

"I KNOW that," she shouted.

"I just take a few notes now and then. You don't mind, do you?"

"Depends on what they are."

"What do you mean?"

"Are they mean, nasty notes, or just ordinary notes?"

"Why?"

"Well, I just thought I'd warn you. Nasty ones are pretty hard to get by with these days."

"Oh, I see what you mean. Thank you for the advice. No, they're quite ordinary notes."

"Nobody ever takes it away from *you*, I bet, do they?"

"What do you mean?"

"Nothing. Let's play."

They played a game. Harriet was wildly bored but she won. Dr. Wagner took a quantity of notes during and after the game.

"I'll bet if you didn't take so many notes, you'd play better."

"Do you think so?"

Harriet looked at him darkly. He couldn't be this stupid. Why was he acting like this?

They played another game. He took less notes and won that game.

"You see!" Harriet was jubilant. "Taking notes all the time makes you no good. Why don't you put that notebook away someplace?" She watched him closely.

He looked faintly amused for the first time. "Suppose," he said slowly, "I give *you* a notebook. Then we'll each have one and we'll be fairly matched." Harriet stared at him hard. Was he kidding her? Was he trying to see what she'd do? Her fingers itched at the thought of a notebook, of a pen flying over the pages, of her thoughts, finally free to move, flowing out. Oh, who cared what he was trying to do.

"Okay, do you have another one?" She tried to appear casual.

"Yes, as a matter of fact, I do." He went to his desk and took out a very pretty little notebook with a bright blue cover. Harriet tried to look unconcerned by looking at the spinet. He also took out a nice little ballpoint pen. He handed both to Harriet. She felt better the moment she had them in her hands.

Dr. Wagner sat down and they began another game. Harriet began to write:

FUNNIEST NOSE I HAVE EVER SEEN. RUNS RIGHT DOWN THE MIDDLE OF HIS FACE LIKE A SNAKE. HE REMINDS ME SOMEWHAT OF PINKY WHITEHEAD BUT HE'S NOT AS REPULSIVE. HE HAS RED HAIR AND FUNNY TEETH. THEY ARE SORT OF YELLOW AND LONG. THIS OFFICE

SMELLS OF CIGARS AND CHALK. I BET HE PLAYS WITH
THOSE TOYS AFTER EVERYONE LEAVES.

Harriet had forgotten all about the game. She suddenly heard Dr. Wagner saying softly, "Harriet . . .
Harriet, it's time to go." She didn't want to leave. I
can't, she thought, live here. She got up quickly and
started for the door.

"Good-by, Harriet," he said gently.

"Good-by," she said. He wasn't a bad sort, she
thought, just a little batty.

Harriet's mother took the notebook away immediately. Harriet felt empty on the ride back.

When she got home her mother disappeared and
the long afternoon stretched ahead of her. Without a
notebook she couldn't spy, she couldn't take notes,
she couldn't play Town, she couldn't do anything. She
was afraid to go and buy another one, and for once
she didn't feel like reading.

She suddenly found herself wondering what would
happen if she went to see Sport and Janie and tried,
privately, to be friendly. After all, being her best
friends, they had always known she was a spy and that
she was going to be a writer, and so how could they
suddenly act as though this were a terrible thing? Maybe they were tired of being mad anyway.

She grabbed her coat and ran down the steps. She
wondered, on the way, if they'd gotten Janie into
dancing school. She could start with that to break the
ice.

The maid let Harriet in and she went up the back
steps straight to Janie's lab. She opened the door and
there stood Janie, so involved in her work that she
didn't even look up.

Harriet said softly, so as not to frighten her, "Janie?"

Janie turned quickly and was so startled that she

208

dripped the test tube she was holding. She stood there absolutely stricken at the sight of Harriet. Then she saw the spreading mess at her feet. "Look what you made me do, just *look!*"

Harriet looked at the floor. Not only was there an awful brown stain spreading rapidly over the parquet, but it also appeared to be burning into the wood.

"What *was* that stuff?"

Janie was busy now, mopping. She didn't say a word, just smiled her terrible smile and cleaned as best she could in silence. The stain was diminished only somewhat after repeated washings. Harriet stood there feeling one of the worst feelings she had ever felt. Janie acted as though she weren't even in the room. A part of the floor was definitely eaten away.

"Maybe we could . . ." Harriet began tentatively.

"Don't you think you've done enough already?" Janie's eyes were nasty.

"I was going to say maybe you could roll the rug over and she wouldn't see." Harriet felt like running out the door.

"So next time you come you can ruin the rug, is that it?"

Harriet looked hard at Janie. Janie stared back at her.

Harriet walked to the door. She kept her back to Janie and didn't say a word because if she had tried to talk she would have cried.

She crossed over to the park and sat down on a bench. She began to reconsider the idea of going to Sport's house. A tear ran down the side of her nose. Janie was one thing, but Sport had always been her best friend. Suppose he acted like Janie?

She waited a minute for some idea to come to her. But there was no way out of it. It was now or never. If Sport was not her friend, then it was better to know it now. Then she would really be alone, and if she were really alone in the world she might as well know it.

She got up from the bench and briskly walked to Sport's house. She ran up the steps to his apartment. As she was getting ready to knock she heard loud laughter from inside, then a giggle from Sport. Out of habit she listened. Sport's father was laughing very hard and saying thing like "WOW" and "How *'bout* that?" Then he said, "How 'bout your ole dad? Now, whadaya think of that? Look at it, Sport, look at that big fat check." Harriet couldn't stand the suspense. She knocked.

Sport came to the door still giggling. When he opened it, he stood there shocked. The smile faded from his face. He looked sad. His father was still running around the room laughing and jumping up and down on furniture. It was funny to stand there looking at Sport with his father running around behind him like a crazy man.

Harriet finally said, "Hi, Sport."

Sport ducked his head as though he had been hit. His eyes went down to the floor, then he backed away a little bit, dragged one foot, and said, "Uh, hello, Harriet." It wasn't much of a welcome, but Harriet pushed right through the door. Sport's father hardly noticed her.

Now he was on the phone jabbering away and waving a check in his hands, "They took it, they took it. It's coming out in the spring! Hey, how 'bout that?"

Harriet looked back at Sport who was still standing holding the door open. "He sold the book?"

In spite of himself a smile broke full across Sport's face. "Yeah," he said reverently, "he just got the check." And then, as though he suddenly remembered, he dropped his eyes to the floor again.

"Hey, Sport, I got to talk to you." Harriet moved

210

toward him the slightest fraction of an inch.

"HOW about THAT?" Sport's father hung up the phone with a bang and, rushing over, hoisted Sport right up on his shoulders. "Wwwooooooowwwww!" he shouted, twirling Sport's body in the air like a tennis racket. Then he swooped him down again and gave him a big hug. "Man! We're in business! Shoes, and a real suit for you, and steak every night. Every night, ole Sport." Sport giggled away happily. "Hi, there, Harriet. I didn't see you. Whatdya think of that? I made it, baby, they're giving me MONEY!"

Harriet laughed up at him. "It's great." Sport's father was a nice-looking man with laughing eyes like Sport and funny hair that fell over his eyes. He always wore an old sweater with holes in it, the same old pair of gray pants, and worn-out sneakers. Sometimes he was gloomy, but when he was happy like this, his smile filled the room. Harriet looked at him with wonder. He was a *writer*. A real *writer*. What did he think? What was in his head? She forgot Sport altogether as she stared at Mr. Rocque. She couldn't resist a question for the notebook. Would he answer something profound?

"What does it feel like to get paid for what you write?" What would he say? She waited breathlessly.

"It's heaven, baby, sheer heaven."

Harriet felt irritated. Was he like everybody else?

"Hey, listen, Sport, get a clean shirt on. I'm taking you out to dinner." Sport ran into his room. "How 'bout you, Harriet? Want to go to dinner with us?"

Before Harriet could say anything, Sport opened the door to his room and shouted "NO" as loud as he could. Then he slammed the door again.

"Well," Sport's father said. He looked embarrassed. "If I know my boy he's trying to get me not to spend that check already."

"I have to go home anyway. I was going to say I

have to go home"—Harriet began to shout—"I couldn't go with you anyway. I couldn't go with you ANYWAY," she screamed toward Sport's door.

"Well," said Sport's father again, looking at Harriet in astonishment. Harriet walked out the door and went home.

That night Harriet had another nightmare. It didn't start out as a nightmare. It started, in fact, as a wonderful dream in which Ole Golly, seated in a rocker and wearing a warm yellow flannel bathrobe, rocked Harriet on her lap as she held her very close.

Harriet's mother came into the room. Harriet was still in her dream, screaming at the top of her lungs, "Ole Golly, Ole Golly, Ole Golly." She kept on crying softly even after her mother was holding her. Then she realized where she was and turned her head to the wall. She pretended to be asleep until her mother left. Then she cried a little more and really fell asleep.

BOOK THREE

CHAPTER 15

When Harriet woke up it seemed very late in the morning. She had been awakened not by her mother calling her but by an angle of the sun hitting her face. She sat straight up in bed. She couldn't hear anything from downstairs. She got up quickly, dressed, and ran down, feeling vaguely as though something was wrong.

No one was in the dining room, in fact the table wasn't even set. She ran down to the kitchen, narrowly missing the cook who dodged aside just in time.

"Where's my breakfast?"

"Lunch, most likely."

"Whatdya mean?"

"It's twelve o'clock. You sure slept a long time."

"Why didn't you wake me up? I'm late for school," Harriet shouted.

"Don't yell at me or I'll quit. Your mama said not to wake you up."

"Where is she?"

"Upstairs. Both of 'em. In there talking about you."

"Where? What do you mean?" Harriet felt frantic.

"Up there." Enjoying herself, the cook gestured upstairs in an offhand way.

Harriet turned and ran up the stairs. The library door was closed. There was the murmur of a voice coming through the door. She crept closer. Then she heard her father talking on the phone. "Well, Dr. Wagner, let me ask you this . . . yes, yes, I know she's a very intelligent child. . . . Yes, well, we're well aware that she has a lot of curiosity. . . . Yes, a sign of intelligence, yes, quite right, I would say so. . . . Now, Doctor, the thing is . . . Yes, I think she just might make a writer. . . . What? a project? oh . . . school . . . yes, I think . . . Yes, we'll call the principal. . . . A few days' absence? Well, I think that can be arranged. . . . But, you're sure, absolutely sure, that she's all right? . . . Yes . . . yes, exceptional . . . Yes, well, I think we know that. . . . What? . . . Oh, yes, well, as I explained, she left . . . But, you think? . . . Yes, I see. . . . Well, I think we have her address somewhere. You think that would be a good idea? . . . I see. . . . Yes, I see. . . . Yes. Well, thank you very much, Doctor. You've been a great deal of help. . . . Yes, I understand, and I agree with you, she always listened to her. . . . Yes, a regression, yes. . . . One thing more, Doctor, you're sure? . . . Yes, quite sure. . . . Good. Well, thank you again. Good-by."

Harriet's ears were standing out from her head. Of course, that's me, she thought. Of course I'm intelligent.

"He thinks we should mumble a mumble to mumble mumble."

Oh, how irritating. When he wasn't shouting into the phone her father couldn't be heard.

"That's a splendid mumble." Mrs. Welsch couldn't be heard either.

"And then the school . . . a mumble. Perhaps a project which would mumble her to mumble herself, and then this mumble wouldn't dominate . . . then more attention, of course . . . but I should call Miss Whitehead and get this mumble started. He's no fink, you know; I think we should listen to him."

"Of course, I think it's all grand. And he says she's not mumble?"

"Not in the least. In fact, quite the mumble. She's an extraordinary mumble and might make a good mumble someday."

How infuriating. Just what one dreams will happen. I've *always* wanted to hear people talk about me, thought Harriet, and now I can't hear it.

Suddenly the doorknob turned. Harriet leaped back but not quickly enough. She decided to make the best of a bad scene. *"BOO,"* she said loudly. Her mother jumped.

"Good Lord, you frightened me. Harriet! What are you doing there? Were you spying on us?"

"Nope. Couldn't hear."

"Oh, well, it's not because you didn't try. Have you had your breakfast?"

"No."

"Then run down and get it. You won't be going to school today, dear—"

"I know. I heard that."

"What else did you hear? Come on, Harriet, out with it." Mrs. Welsch closed the door quickly as she heard Mr. Welsch say, "Hello, Miss Whitehead?"

"Nothing," Harriet said.

"Honest?"

"Honest."

"All right, run along and eat, then. I have to write a letter."

I wonder, thought Harriet, what is up?

She was still wondering two days later and no wiser. She had had time to catch up on a lot of spy work, but she was surprised to find that on the third day away from school she was beginning to miss it. She had covered her spy route in the first two days, giving ample time to each case, but there really hadn't been much going on. Little Joe Curry was reinstated after he said he was just hungry. This touched the heart of Mama Dei Santi. The next day, however, he was caught with a whole ham. Harriet was there when this happened. It was very exciting because not only was he caught stealing the ham but he was caught at the instant he was giving it to three of the happiest-looking children anybody ever saw. Harriet wrote in her notebook:

THAT WAS A SCENE I'M GLAD I SAW BECAUSE I WOULD HAVE GUESSED THAT MAMA DEI SANTI WOULD HAVE BOPPED HIM OVER THE HEAD BUT WHEN SHE SAW THE CHILDREN SHE BURST INTO TEARS AND COMMENCED WAILING AND GIVING THE KIDS EVERYTHING IN SIGHT. EVEN A WHOLE LONG SALAMI. THEN SHE SHOOED THEM AWAY AND TOLD THEM NOT TO COME BACK OR SHE'D CALL THE COPS. PEOPLE ARE VERY FUNNY. ALSO SHE DIDN'T FIRE LITTLE JOE. SHE TOLD HIM HE BETTER SEE A DOCTOR. HE EATS TOO MUCH.

Mrs. Plumber was told by her doctor that she could get up. As far as Harriet could see she hadn't hit the bed since, but flew from one party to the next all day, did charity work incessantly, and, according to her phone conversations the next day, stayed out half the night too.

The Robinsons showed a lot of people their doll.

The Dei Santi family, other than the incident with Little Joe, had a fairly uneventful week. Fabio was working hard, even harder than Bruno. Franca flunked some test or other and came home in tears. Dino, the baby, got the chicken pox, so Mama Dei Santi had to stay at home with him.

The most surprising thing was Harrison Withers. Harriet went by expecting to see him moping about his cats, and there he was humming and working on a cage in the happiest way possible. She couldn't understand it. He even got up and ate some lunch. He actually made himself a tuna fish sandwich and had a coke. Harriet leaned back against the wall and wrote:

I JUST CAN'T UNDERSTAND THIS. OH, I KNOW, MAYBE HE DIDN'T HAVE ENOUGH MONEY TO EAT GOOD BEFORE BECAUSE HE HAD TO BUY ALL THOSE KIDNEYS. OR MAYBE HE COULDN'T EVER EAT TUNA AND HE LIKES TUNA. MAYBE THE CATS ALWAYS GRABBED IT.

She leaned over the parapet again to study the problem at length. Harrison Withers was humming away, even tapping his foot as he worked. She watched, puzzled, until suddenly he looked up in the direction of the kitchen door. Then she saw it. Into the room, as though he owned it, to the accompaniment of loud cooing and baby talk from Harrison Withers walked the tiniest cat Harriet had ever seen. It was a funny-looking little black-and-white kitten which had a mustache which made it look as though it were sneering. It stopped, looked at Harrison Withers as though he were a curiosity, and then walked disdainfully across the room. Harrison Withers watched in adoration. Harriet leaned back and wrote:

SO THAT'S IT. WONDER WHERE HE GOT THAT CAT. I GUESS IF YOU WANT A CAT YOU RUN INTO ONE SOMEPLACE. HEE HEE. THEY AIN'T GOING TO CHANGE HARRISON WITHERS.

And, for some reason, as she walked home Harriet felt unaccountably happy.

On the third day Harriet woke up and found herself really wishing she were going to school. She didn't say anything to her mother, however, because she didn't want to go *that* much. In the afternoon she decided to go and see what was happening at the clubhouse. She waited until time for school to be out, then she went over and crawled over the fence to her post. Rachel came home, bringing Marion Hawthorne with her. They walked sedately.

They walk like old ladies, thought Harriet.

"Rachel, don't you think it would be nice if we could play bridge in the afternoons?" Marion had a kind of cawing voice, like a crow.

"Well," said Rachel, "I don't know how...."

"Oh, that's easy. I've watched my mother lots of times," said Marion authoritatively. "Why don't we play Mahjong? I like that."

"Well, I think bridge is *MUCH chic*-er, but if you want to we will. Do you have a set?"

"Yes. That is, Mother does."

Bridge? Mahjong? thought Harriet. Who are they kidding? Wait till Sport hears about this.

Beth Ellen arrived. Rachel and Marion nodded curtly in her direction. "I think," said Marion, "that we should uphold a certain standard in this club."

"Yes?" said Rachel, although she looked as though she hadn't the foggiest idea what Marion was getting at.

"Don't you, Beth Ellen?" Marion asked pointedly.

"Ye-s." This came out very small.

"I mean, I think we have to be very careful who we take in . . . and"—she looked around darkly—"who we *KEEP* in."

"Oh," said Beth Ellen, "you mean like a country club."

"Yes," said Marion, "exactly. I think that anyone who wants to have a social life in the afternoon should be welcome, that is—" she added mysteriously, "that is if they're the right kind of person."

"Yes," said Rachel.

"Yes," whispered Beth Ellen.

"I also think and I don't know how you'll feel about this"—Marion drew herself up until she looked like her mother— "but I feel that in view of the fact that I'm the class officer I should be president of the club."

Well, thought Harriet, it's a good thing for you I'm not in this club, because you'd get it, right across the head.

"I therefore nominate myself for president."

"I second it," said Rachel. She must second things in her sleep, thought Harriet.

"Motion carried," screeched Beth Ellen in a fit of helpless giggles.

Marion frowned Beth Ellen into silence. "Now that that's settled, I shall make a few decisions. First, I think we should serve tea."

"My mother isn't going to like that," said Rachel.

"Well, not really tea, just milk in tea cups. We DO have to *LEARN*, you know."

"She isn't going to like that either. The cup part."

"Well, we can each bring our own cup. Second, we have to set up a card table and chairs. Third"—she stood up and pointed her finger as though she were knighting them—"I make you vice president, Rachel, and you are the secretary-treasurer, Beth Ellen."

"What do I have to do?" Beth Ellen looked terrified.

"You take minutes, collect the money, and serve the tea."

"Oh."

In other words, thought Harriet, everything.

"I think also we should discuss people who have the wrong attitude." Marion was liking her job more and more. "I think we were all aware at the last meeting of a very wrong attitude coming from Sport and Janie."

Naturally, you idiot, thought Harriet. Wait till they find out you're president. Just as the others began to arrive from school a sudden rainstorm drove them into the clubhouse. Harriet watched a minute to see Sport and Janie run across the yard, the last ones to arrive. Then Harriet ran with all her might, but she was still soaked through by the time she got home.

Upstairs, when she had pulled off her wet spy clothes and gotten into her bathrobe, she wrote a long account of what she had seen, adding at the end:

MARION HAWTHORNE IS TOO BIG FOR HER BRITCHES. SHE'S GOING TO GET IT.

Three days later Harriet was bored to extinction. She had played Town all morning in her room and she was beginning, for the first time in her life, to be bored with her own mind. She was just about to throw her notebook across the room when she heard the doorbell ring. She jumped up and ran as fast as she could downstairs. Her mother was at the front door taking a Special Delivery letter from the postman.

"What's that?" asked Harriet eagerly.

"Well . . . I do believe," said her mother scrutinizing the letter, "that's it's a letter for you, Harriet." Her mother smiled at her.

"Who from?"

"Why, I haven't the faintest idea," her mother said casually, and handing Harriet the letter, disappeared into the library.

I never get letters, thought Harriet, and tore open the envelope. She recognized the handwriting at once.

Dear Harriet,

I have been thinking about you and I have decided that if you are ever going to be a writer it is time you got cracking. You are eleven years old and haven't written a thing but notes. Make a story out of some of those notes and send it to me.

"'Beauty is truth, truth beauty,'—that is all
Ye know on earth, and all ye need to know."

John Keats. And don't you ever forget it.

Now in case you ever run into the following problem, I want to tell you about it. Naturally, you put down the truth in your notebooks. What would be the point if you didn't? And naturally those notebooks should not be read by anyone else, but if they are, then, Harriet, you are going to have to do two things, and you don't like either one of them:

1) You have to apologize.
2) You have to lie.

Otherwise you are going to lose a friend. Little lies that make people feel better are not bad, like thanking someone for a meal they made even if you hated it, or telling a sick person they look better when they don't, or someone with a hideous new hat that it's lovely. Remember that writing is to put love in the world, not to use against your friends. But to yourself you must tell the truth.

Another thing. If you're missing me I want you to know I'm not missing you. Gone is gone. I never miss anything or anyone because it, all becomes a lovely memory. I guard my memories and love them, but I don't get in them and lie down. You can even make stories from yours, but remember, they don't come back. Just think how awful it would be if they did. You don't need me now. You're eleven years old which is old enough to get busy at growing up to be the person you want to be.

No more nonsense.
Ole Golly Waldenstein

When she finished reading, Harriet had a wide grin

on her face. She ran upstairs holding the letter like a treasure found on the beach. She ran into her room, sat at the desk, and read it over twice. Then she took out some clean paper and a pen. She sat holding the pen over the paper. Nothing happened. She referred to her notes. Still nothing happened. Then she jumped up, ran down to the library, and lugged her father's typewriter up the steps. With a great deal of effort she hoisted it up to her desk. The first piece of paper she tried to put in got jammed and too wrinkled to write on. She tore it up and put in another. Then she started to type furiously.

Harriet went back to school the next day. It felt like the beginning of term again. She strolled down the empty halls, considerably late because she wanted to make a grand entrance. Her mother and father hadn't been there when she got up, so she decided to sneak off to school. Enough is enough, she thought to herself as she was walking past the principal's office. She decided suddenly to make a note of how she felt, so she wedged herself into a little niche usually reserved for a piece of sculpture.

ENOUGH IS ENOUGH. IT IS TIME TO RISE AND SHINE. WAIT TILL THE NEW YORKER GETS A LOAD OF THAT STORY. IT WAS HARD MAKING UP HIM FINDING THE CAT BUT I THINK I MADE UP A GOOD MORAL—THAT IS THAT SOME PEOPLE ARE ONE WAY AND SOME PEOPLE ARE ANOTHER AND THAT'S THAT.

The door to the principal's office opened and Harriet looked up. To her horror she saw her mother and father walk out. She ducked back into the niche. Maybe, she thought, if I don't breathe, I'll look like a statue. She held her breath and her mother and father walked past without seeing her. They were laughing and looking at each other, so that even though she rolled her eyes at them they didn't notice.

"Boy, wait'll she hears that!" her father was saying.

"She'll be, I'm afraid, impossible to live with," her mother said, grinning.

"You know what?" said Mr. Welsch. "I bet she'll do a good job."

They went out the front door and Harriet let out a huge breath. I almost burst, she thought. She scrambled down and ran for her classroom. When she got there everything was in total confusion because Miss Elson wasn't in the room. Everyone was throwing things at everyone else, including wads of chewing gum, and Marion Hawthorne was at the front desk screeching herself blue for order. No one paid the slightest bit of attention to her but went on with such chaos that Harriet was able to slip gratefully into her seat unnoticed. At home she had thought about making some spectacular entrance, perhaps in a funny hat, but when she got to the door she had been stricken with terror and now was glad she hadn't. She sat there quietly looking at everyone screaming and running around like nuts. She wrote in her notebook:

I AM GOING TO WRITE A STORY ABOUT THESE PEOPLE. THEY ARE JUST BATS. HALF OF THEM DON'T EVEN HAVE A PROFESSION.

Miss Elson came in and there was instant silence. Everyone trooped to his desk. Sport looked like he would faint when he saw Harriet, and Janie smiled an evil smile at her. No one else seemed to notice. Miss Elson stood up.

"Well, I'm glad to see that you're back with us, Harriet." She smiled sweetly in Harriet's direction and ten necks swiveled like keys turning in locks. Harriet tried to smile at Miss Elson and glare at the others, but this being impossible, she got an idiotic look on her face.

"I'm particularly glad," continued Miss Elson, "because I have a special announcement to make about a change in school policy."

What in the world, thought Harriet, does that have to do with me?

"You are aware that we have always let you elect your class officer and that the class officer has always automatically been the editor of the Sixth Grade Page. However we have decided that this is too much work for one person . . ."

Marion Hawthorne gasped audibly.

". . . and have therefore decided that hereinafter the teacher will select someone else to be editor.

"We have made this choice on the basis of ability. In looking over all the compositions handed in by the class, Miss Whitehead and I have decided that several of you have a flair for writing and that these few should take turns having the editorship. The selection has been made, and the editor from now on for this half year"—she paused dramatically and smiled—"will be Harriet M. Welsch."

You could have heard a pin drop. Harriet stared at Miss Elson in disbelief. They all looked at Miss Elson. No one looked at Harriet. "Harriet has been chosen," she continued, "for the first half of the year and Beth Ellen for the second half. That means Harriet will write the page for this semester and Beth Ellen next semester. The others will have their chance next year."

Beth Ellen turned beet-red and almost passed out. Harriet looked around her. Everyone was looking around at either her or Beth Ellen, which was causing Beth Ellen untold embarrassment. There seemed to be a general uneasiness in the room.

Miss Elson looked unconcerned, and picking up a

textbook, she said, "And now today, children, we have studied—"

"Miss Elson"—Marion Hawthorne was on her feet—"I want to register a protest with the school on behalf of a group which I happen to be president of and which, by general agreement, has decided that this decision is unfair to the class, the great majority which belong—"

"*Of* which, Marion," Miss Elson corrected.

"—to this club OF which I am president. Now, therefore—"

"That's enough, Marion, sit down. I think you have made yourself clear. I would like to know when you have had the time, however, to amass this great tide of public opinion. I didn't see you asking anyone after I spoke." Marion sat there unable to think of a thing.

"I think, therefore, just to enlighten you as to the opinions of your following, and for no other reason, that we should take a vote. I want to make it perfectly clear that the only thing this vote will elicit is a talk with Miss Whitehead. I doubt very seriously that it is at all possible to change the decision. I am sure it is too late. But I do think we might make this an interesting experiment in terms of democracy. It has long been my opinion that one *never* knows the outcome of a vote no matter *how* sure we think we are. And Marion seems terribly sure. I think we should see, therefore. Now I want hands raised on how many want Harriet and Beth Ellen to take over for this year."

Marion and Rachel clenched their hands firmly to their sides as though they might rise of their own accord. Marion actually sat on hers.

Harriet and Beth Ellen naturally voted for themselves, Harriet's arm flying up like a Nazi salute and Beth Ellen's creeping tentatively and trembling as though she were waving.

Two and two, thought Harriet.

Sport's hand went up. He thinks what Marion writes is stupid, thought Harriet; it has nothing to do with being on my side. Janie's hand went up. Same for her, thought Harriet; she just wants to be able to read the paper.

Laura Peters, Pinky Whitehead, and The Boy with the Green Socks did not have their hands up.

Uh-oh, thought Harriet, that makes five to four. Or have they just not decided? Where is Carrie Andrews? Absent today.

Very slowly, and in his own particular creepy way, Pinky Whitehead put his hand up. Well, thought Harriet, I never thought I'd see the day when Pinky Whitehead would save my life. He looked back at her. She gave him a radiant smile and felt like a first class hypocrite.

"That," said Miss Elson, "decides that. I think we can learn from this, children, and particularly Marion, not to count your eggs before they vote for you." Beth Ellen giggled helplessly, then stopped and looked around at everyone as though suddenly aware of her responsibilities.

CHAPTER 16

Harriet got out the first edition in record time. When she took in her finished page, the senior who was chief editor said that it was the fastest she had ever seen anyone write.

On the day the paper appeared, Harriet was horribly nervous. Suppose, she thought on her way to school, I stink? Suppose everyone looks at each other and says, Why did we ever get rid of Marion Hawthorne? Maybe she wasn't Dostoievsky, but she was readable at least. Suppose—Harriet bit her lip in her musing—they insist on a recount. She was trembling by the time she got to class.

Everyone at every desk had a paper. Everyone had his nose buried in the Sixth Grade Page. Harriet couldn't bear to look around. She slid into her seat and guiltily started looking at her own copy which had been put there.

She read her own printed words with a mixture of horror and joy.

MRS. AGATHA K. PLUMBER IS A RICH LADY ON EAST

END AVENUE WHO THOUGHT SHE HAD FOUND OUT THE
SECRET OF LIFE WHICH WAS TO STAY IN BED ALL THE
TIME. SHE IS A VERY STUPID LADY. THEN LO AND BE-
HOLD THE DOCTOR TOLD HER SHE HAD TO STAY IN BED
AND SHE FAINTED AWAY IN SURPRISE. THEN HE TOLD
HER HE HAD MADE A MISTAKE, AND SHE HASN'T HIT THE
BED SINCE. I THINK HE TRICKED HER BECAUSE SHE
THOUGHT SHE WANTED TO STAY IN BED WHICH IS
STUPID. WHICH GOES TO SHOW YOU TWO THINGS—
THAT WHAT YOU WANT IS MAYBE STUPID AND THAT
DOCTORS ARE FINKS.

Harriet felt in rereading that it had a strong ring to
it. She looked around at everybody reading. They are
only looking for mistakes, she thought. I wonder what
each one is reading. I wonder if writers ever see anyone reading their books, on the subway maybe. She
turned back to the paper. She had had a hard time
deciding between a story about Fabio and a story
about the Robinsons. She had finally decided to do a
story about Franca Dei Santi because she was closer
in age to the class and therefore might interest them
more.

FRANCA DEI SANTI HAS ONE OF THE DUMBEST FACES
YOU COULD EVER HOPE TO SEE. I DON'T KNOW HOW SHE
GETS THROUGH THE DAY. SHE EVEN HAS TO LEAN ON
THINGS ALL THE TIME. SHE IS ABOUT OUR AGE AND GOES
TO A PUBLIC SCHOOL WHERE SHE IS ALWAYS FLUNKING
THINGS LIKE SHOP THAT WE DON'T HAVE. MAYBE
THEY TEACH THEM HOW TO RUN A SHOP THERE. ANY-
WAY IT WON'T DO FRANCA A BIT OF GOOD BECAUSE SHE
WON'T EVER LEARN ANYTHING ANYWAY. HER FATHER
OWNS A STORE ON EIGHTY-SIXTH AND ANYONE WHO
WANTS TO CAN GO ANY DAY AND LOOK THROUGH THE
BACK WINDOW AND SEE FRANCA. SHE IS THE SHORTEST
GIRL THERE AND IS ALWAYS MOONING AROUND. YOU

WOULD KNOW HER ANYWHERE. ONE DAY I SAW FRANCA
ON THE STREET. SHE WAS WALKING ALONG IN FRONT
OF ME DRAGGING HER FEET. I KNEW IT WAS HER BE-
CAUSE SHE ALWAYS HANGS HER HEAD OVER TO ONE
SIDE. I DON'T KNOW WHY. MAYBE IT'S TOO HEAVY.
ANYWAY I WATCHED HER AND SHE DID THE DUMBEST
THING. SHE WENT INTO THE PARK AND STRAIGHT OVER
TO SOME PIGEONS. THEY LOOKED LIKE THEY WERE
EXPECTING HER. THEN SHE HAD A LONG CONVERSATION
WITH THOSE PIGEONS. I HID BEHIND A TREE AND I STILL
COULDN'T HEAR A WORD BUT FRANCA LOOKED LIKE SHE
WAS HAVING A GOOD TIME. SHE DOESN'T HAVE A GOOD
TIME AT HOME BECAUSE EVERYONE KNOWS HOW DUMB
SHE IS AND DOESN'T TALK TO HER.

By the time Harriet finished reading, Miss Elson
had walked in. Harriet watched everyone put their
papers away. Each one looked at Harriet surreptitious-
ly as they did so, but she couldn't tell anything by
their faces. They just looked at her curiously.

She noticed, however, that at lunchtime all the noses
were stuck in the paper again.

That night at dinner Harriet suddenly felt like one
big ear. Every single thing her mother and father said
seemed to be important. Some of the things she didn't
understand, but they were none the less intriguing.

"I really don't understand Mabel Gibbs. She starts
out with this big thing about the kids going to dancing school—you'd think from the way she talked that
they would be absolute apes in the drawing room if
we didn't send them—and I told her at the time, of
course, that I thought Harriet was too young. *Naturally,* she's *going* to dancing school but I think twelve
is perhaps a better age, that's all. Well, then, after all
that, Mabel says to me ever so calmly the other day,
'I just don't think that Janie is ready yet.' Can you
imagine?"

"She wants to save the money," interjected Harriet.

"Harriet, you mustn't say such things," said Mrs. Welsch.

"Why shouldn't she? It's the God's truth," said Mr. Welsch.

"Well, we don't *know* that. She said, in fact, that she couldn't do a thing with Janie and she just didn't want the job of having to force her into a black velvet dress every Friday night. It just wasn't worth it. She's hoping Janie will change suddenly—"

"Into a pumpkin," said Harriet.

"Into a lady," continued Mrs. Welsch.

"Time enough for that," said Mr. Welsch.

"You know, I was thinking the other day"—Mrs. Welsch seemed to be changing the subject—"that Milly Andrews really hasn't got good sense. Did you see her at the Peters' party? Well, I don't know what *you* were doing. *Everybody* was talking about it. Jack Peters was stoned out of his mind and falling off the bar stool, and there was Milly Andrews just smiling at him like an idiot."

Mr. Welsch said nothing. He was swallowing. He was about to speak, when the phone rang. He threw his napkin down and stood up. "That better be from the *Times*. If they don't print that retraction tomorrow I'm going to be mad as a hornet."

He stormed angrily to the telephone.

"What's a retraction?" asked Harriet.

"Well, it's like this. If a newspaper makes a mistake and they are told about it, then they print the fact that they have made a mistake and at the same time they print the correct information."

"Oh," said Harriet. That night when she went up to bed she took copious notes. Later, under the covers, she read a book on newspaper reporting that she had found in the school library.

* * *

In the next edition of the paper the Sixth Grade Page carried the following items:

JANIE GIBBS HAS WON HER BATTLE. THIS SHOULD BE A LESSON TO ALL OF YOU IN COURAGE AND DETER-MINATION. IF YOU DON'T KNOW WHAT I'M TALKING ABOUT, THEN ASK HER.

JACK PETERS (LAURA PETERS' FATHER) WAS STONED OUT OF HIS MIND AT THE PETERS' PARTY LAST SAT-URDAY NIGHT. MILLY ANDREWS (CARRIE ANDREWS' MOTHER) JUST SMILED AT HIM LIKE AN IDIOT.

FOR ANYONE WHO DOESN'T KNOW IT, A RETRACTION MEANS THAT A NEWSPAPER IS CORRECTING ITS MIS-TAKES. SO FAR THIS PAGE HASN'T MADE ANY MIS-TAKES.

During the ensuing weeks the following entries held the class enthralled.

MR. HARRY WELSCH ALMOST LOST HIS JOB LAST WEEK FOR BEING LATE. HE IS ALWAYS SLOW IN THE MORNING.

ASK CARRIE ANDREWS IF SHE FEELS ALL RIGHT.

And a week later:

ASK LAURA PETERS IF ALL IS WELL AT HOME.

MISS ELSON WAS TRAILED HOME FROM SCHOOL THE

OTHER DAY AND IT TURNS OUT SHE LIVES IN A REAL RAT HOLE OF AN APARTMENT. MAYBE THE SCHOOL DOESN'T PAY HER ENOUGH MONEY TO LIVE IN A GOOD PLACE. THERE WILL BE A SIZZLING EDITORIAL ON THIS NEXT WEEK.

A very hot item was:

THERE ARE CERTAIN PEOPLE IN A CERTAIN CLUB WHO OUGHT TO WATCH OUT BECAUSE THERE ARE CERTAIN OTHER PEOPLE WHO WANT TO TAKE OVER FROM CERTAIN OTHER PEOPLE BECAUSE CERTAIN OTHER PEOPLE DON'T WANT TO SPEND ALL AFTERNOON DRINKING TEA AND PLAYING A CERTAIN GAME.

After this last item Harriet watched the group very carefully. She detected a touch of uneasiness, but nothing actively happened at school.

She went therefore that afternoon to spy on the clubhouse. She was completely gratified by what she saw and heard. Marion, Rachel, Laura, Carrie, The Boy with the Green Socks, and Pinky Whitehead were all there by the time she got there. A discussion was in progress.

"Well, it's just outrageous," said Marion in a huff.

"Scandalous," echoed Rachel.

"The things she writes anyway are just absurd," continued Marion. "Whoever heard of such a thing in a newspaper? When I ran that paper no one read things like that. Things like that don't belong in a paper. She should be stopped."

"I like reading them," said Pinky.

That's Pinky, thought Harriet.

"She can't be stopped," said Carrie. "She's the editor."

"Even so," said Marion, "somebody should." She

234

paused dramatically. *"We* should."

"But what was she talking about? About the club, I mean," asked Pinky.

Marion, Rachel, Laura, and Carrie all looked into the distance. Obviously, thought Harriet, those four play bridge.

"Uh-oh," said Marion, "here comes trouble."

Sport and Janie appeared at the back door. They were both furious. They walked across the yard like a pair of Gestapo agents come to question.

"I think," said Janie, "that we had better have this out."

"This has gone far enough," said Sport and looked at Pinky and The Boy with the Green Socks. "I can't imagine what you MEN think you're doing here."

"What? What?" said both boys together.

"Well, think about it," continued Sport. "How many men play bridge in the afternoon?"

"My father plays bridge," said Pinky defensively.

"But not in the afternoon," sneered Janie. "He plays bridge at *night*."

"When he's *forced* to," said Sport.

"What"—Marion stood up—"are you two talking about?"

"You know perfectly well what," said Sport. "You've been rattling around here with tea cups and packs of cards for two weeks now, and why we even listened to you for one minute I don't know because we have just as much right in this club as you do."

"Well, I am PRESIDENT."

"Oh, no, you're not, as of now," said Janie.

Beth Ellen sidled in. Janie flung her a long look. "And you're not secretary-treasurer either."

Beth Ellen spoke up suddenly. "I don't give a hang. I never wanted to be and besides I *hate* bridge."

Everyone stared at her because it was the longest

sentence she had ever been heard to say.

"People," said Marion in a slow, hard way, "who do not belong, can LEAVE."

"This is our clubhouse too," shouted Sport. "You couldn't even have BUILT it without me."

"Precisely," said Janie, "and I think the point is we should discuss exactly what this club is supposed to be for."

There was a long silence. Some of them kicked the dirt with their feet. Others looked at the sky. Harriet suddenly noticed that Rachel was giving Janie a long hateful look. Finally Rachel said, "It may be your CLUB but it's my BACKYARD."

The remark fell heavily into the group. What now? thought Harriet with excitement.

"That," said Janie finally, "settles that." She turned and walked toward the back door.

"You bet your nose it does," said Sport and followed Janie. They slammed the back door, producing a distant shriek from Mrs. Hennessey.

"I agree with them," said Beth Ellen and stomped out. What in the world has happened to Beth Ellen? thought Harriet. She's not a mouse anymore. Harriet watched with glee as one by one the other children left. Marion and Rachel finally sat alone. They looked at each other and then looked away.

"I guess," said Rachel with some embarrassment, "that I'll go see if the cake is ready." She was getting up rather forlornly when suddenly Laura and Carrie came back.

"We decided that there wasn't anything else to do anyway, so we might as well play bridge," said Laura.

"Besides," said Carrie, "I'm rather fond of it."

Harriet watched while they set up a dinky little card table, put out some chipped cups, and cut the cake. When they dealt the cards, she left. As she went over the fence she thought to herself, I'm glad

236

my life is different. I bet they'll be doing that the rest of their lives—and she felt rather sorry for them for a moment. But only for a moment. As she walked along the street she thought, I have a nice life. With or without Ole Golly, I have a nice life.

The time is ripe, Harriet thought as she went into the senior editor's office. She had a long private conversation with the senior editor, who was called Lisa Quackenbush. She was a tallish girl who spit a lot when she talked and who seemed to find Harriet as funny as a TV comedian. Harriet couldn't see anything funny whatever in what she was relating to Miss Quakenbush and so made some rapid notes after leaving the office.

MISS QUACKENBUSH IS EITHER INSANE OR SHE HAS A VERY NERVOUS LAUGH.

The week after the conference there appeared on the Sixth Grade Page the following announcement. It was placed quite prominently in the center of the page with a border around it.

THIS PAGE WISHES TO RETRACT CERTAIN STATEMENTS PRINTED IN A CERTAIN NOTEBOOK BY THE EDITOR OF THE SIXTH GRADE PAGE WHICH WERE UNFAIR STATEMENTS AND BESIDES WERE LIES. ANYONE WHO SAW THESE STATEMENTS IS HEREBY NOTIFIED THAT THEY WERE LIES AND THAT A GENERAL APOLOGY IS OFFERED BY THE EDITOR OF THE SIXTH GRADE PAGE.

The day the announcement appeared Harriet stayed home from sheer embarrassment. She managed to convince her mother that she was just about to come down with a terrible cold, the type of cold that could be nipped in the bud by only one little day home from school. There is, of course, no kind of a cold in the world like this, but Harriet's mother had become convinced of this because it had happened to work so many times. Harriet knew just what signs of listlessness it took to put her mother's mind into this track. She languished, therefore, until she heard her mother leave to go shopping. The moment the door shut Harriet leaped from the bed as though shot from a cannon.

She worked all day on her story, that is from ten in the morning until three in the afternoon. Then she got up, stretched, and feeling very virtuous, she took a walk by the river. There was a cold wind off the water, but the day was one of those bright, brilliant, shining days that made her feel the world was beautiful, would always be, would always sing, could hold no disappointments.

She skipped along the bank, stopping once to watch a tugboat, following an old woman once all the way to the mayor's house. She took a few notes, concentrating on description which she felt to be her weakest point.

YESTERDAY WHEN I WENT INTO THAT HARDWARE STORE IT SMELLED LIKE THE INSIDE OF AN OLD THERMOS BOTTLE.

I HAVE THOUGHT A LOT ABOUT BEING THINGS SINCE TRYING TO BE AN ONION. I HAVE TRIED TO BE A BENCH IN THE PARK, AN OLD SWEATER, A CAT, AND MY MUG IN THE BATHROOM. I THINK I DID THE MUG BEST BECAUSE WHEN I WAS LOOKING AT IT I FELT IT LOOKING BACK AT ME AND I FELT LIKE WE WERE TWO MUGS LOOKING AT EACH OTHER. I WONDER IF GRASS TALKS.

She sat there thinking, feeling very calm, happy, and immensely pleased with her own mind. She looked up and down the walk. No one was in sight. She looked

238

out over the water to the neon sign whose pink greed spoiled the view at night. When she looked back she saw them coming toward her. They were moving so slowly they hardly seemed to be in motion. Sport had his hands in his pockets and looked out over the water. Janie walked with her eyes as nearly skyward as possible. If there had been anything in front of her she would have broken her neck. They didn't appear to be talking, but they were so far away Harriet couldn't really tell.

They were so far away that they looked like dolls.

They made her think of the way she imagined the people when she played Town. Somehow this way she could see them better than she ever had before. She looked at them each carefully in the longish time it took them to reach her. She made herself walk in Sport's shoes, feeling the holes in his socks rub against his ankles. She pretended she had an itchy nose when Janie put one abstracted hand up to scratch. She felt what it would feel like to have freckles and yellow hair like Janie, then funny ears and skinny shoulders like Sport.

When they reached her they just stood there in front of her, each looking in a different direction. The wind was terribly cold. Harriet looked at their feet. They looked at her feet. Then they looked at their own feet.

Well, thought Harriet. She opened her notebook very carefully, watching their eyes as she did. They watched her back. She wrote:

OLE GOLLY IS RIGHT. SOMETIMES YOU HAVE TO LIE.

She looked up at Sport and Janie. They didn't look angry. They were just waiting for her to finish. She continued:

NOW THAT THINGS ARE BACK TO NORMAL I CAN GET SOME REAL WORK DONE.

She slammed the book and stood up. All three of them turned then and walked along the river.